THE STORM

And

Other Short Stories

THE STORM

AND

OTHER SHORT STORIES

ESTHER CHILTON

THE STORM

Copyright © Esther Chilton 2023

The right of Esther Chilton to be identified as
author of this work has been
asserted by her in accordance with sections 77 and
78 of the Copyright, Designs
and Patents Act 1988.

All rights reserved. No part of this publication may be reproduced, stored in any retrieval system, copied in any form or by any means, electronic, mechanical, photocopying, recording or otherwise, without written permission from the author. You must not circulate this book in any format.

This is a work of fiction. Names, characters, places and incidents either are products of the author's imagination or are used fictitiously. Any resemblance to actual events, or locales, or persons, living or dead, is entirely coincidental.

For all those writers who doubt themselves -

Never give up; believe in yourself

Contents

The Storm	9
Daffodils	11
Blue-Eyed Boy	17
The Diary of Ellie Carter, Aged 6 ¾	21
Love Lost	23
Cream Scones	28
A Child's Dream	34
A New Friend	50
First Sight	54
Mystery Mayhem	55
In Search of Dinosaurs	61
Fairies	70
The Escape	74
A Special Helper	78
The Return	84

The Hacker	87
Stranger	94
The Holiday	101
Richard Edwards	107
The Dark Place	110
Acknowledgements	116
About The Author	117

THE STORM

Carrie tried not to scream. She gripped the side of the boat, willing it to stay upright. It bounced on the monstrous waves, hurling her from side to side. She looked up at the clouds, mounting and darkening in colour with every passing second. A storm. Not now. *Not now*!

It had all started so well. The shimmering waters had been peaceful, the waves lapping gently at the side of the boat. She'd clasped the treasure map in her hand, images of golden cups and dazzling diamonds filling her head as she scanned the horizon searching for land. And there it was! Though it was still some distance away and the sun had slowly slunk away, the clouds shielding its fierce yellow and orange glow. She'd reached for the lantern, her eyes fighting against the gathering gloom. She hadn't expected a storm. Perhaps it was the treasure's curse. Maybe that was why no one had ever found it – and no one ever would… She shivered, pushing the thought aside.

What was that? Not a hole at the bottom? Water sloshed at her feet, gaining momentum, splashing her arms and face, cold and chilling to her sweat-soaked skin.

Now the boat was spinning, swirling round and round, like a whirlpool about to suck her in. Carrie closed her eyes and held her breath. Surely it couldn't end this way?

A hand touched her shoulder. Someone had come

to save her. Her eyes flew open and she looked into brown ones just like her own, but stern.

She listened to the hiss as the rubber dingy deflated and followed the stony eyes to the ocean of the paddling pool, now devoid of water, and on to the sopping wet, newly mown lawn. Perhaps it was time to go inside.

DAFFODILS

I pick a pretty daffodil from the vase on the side. But then, they're all pretty, aren't they, Jenny? I gently stroke the soft silken surface of the flower and tears stream down my face. Daffodils were always your favourite.

They were just coming into bloom on the day you were born. I was standing outside Mrs Farmer's house at the time. It had been such a miserable morning with fog, rain, sleet, even some snow, everything apart from sunshine. But Mrs Farmer's daffodils made everything sunny. And then my waters broke. I forgot all about daffodils after that. But you didn't, did you, Jenny?

On a bright spring day, we would often take a trip to the park. We'd pass the sea of yellow in Mrs Farmer's garden along the way.

"Daffs, daffs," you would shout, your chubby arms pointing and a huge grin on your face.

You were always such a sunny child, like your favourite flower. We didn't have a lot in those days. Your father hadn't long left us. It turned out he had been seeing Mrs Charlton at number seven for the past year. So it was a bit of a struggle for the two of us all on our own. But we survived, Jenny, you and I.

You loved the dolls and dresses I made you and poorly panda bear, as you named him. Knitting was never my strong point, but you didn't care. You loved them all. You always followed me round, doll or panda in one hand and a duster in the other, replenishing the sticky marks I had just wiped away.

But best of all, you loved the big outside. It was such a shame we didn't have a garden of our own. That's the thing about flats. So we went out instead, especially to the park. You loved the swings. Swings and looking at everyone's best blooms bursting with colour. Mrs Farmer's garden was the best. She used to be on the television. I'd marvel at her, always performing miracles with someone's mud and mayhem of a garden.

When you were a little bit older, you walked to the park. You always stopped outside Mrs Farmer's house. Your eyes would mist over and I could see you imagining yourself in her garden, tiptoeing through the daffodils and glorious greens, stopping every now and then to smell or pick a flower that took your fancy. You would twirl round and round, a princess in her own secret garden.

"The daffodils have gone," you said one day, squinting against the brilliance of the spring sunshine as it merged into early summer.

I smiled and told you tales of the changing seasons. I showed you pictures of roses and we bought an African violet for the windowsill. You took charge of the watering. But it was always daffodils you wanted.

"Look at the daffodils, Mum. Look, one's come out," you said, standing outside Mrs Farmer's the following February. "Can I hold it? Can I?"

"No, don't be silly, Jenny. It's Mrs Farmer's," I said, horrified. "We can't just pick daffodils from anyone's garden."

"I'm sure she wouldn't mind, Mum." You looked up at me with those brown eyes, swirling like melting chocolate.

"No," I said, my final word on the matter.

Why didn't I let you have the daffodil? Would it have hurt to take just one? I would let you have every single one of them if I could exchange them for all the pain you suffered. It's so easy to look back and wish things had been different.

But I didn't know. You were only ten. You were looking forward to going to the big school in the autumn, to being in the school play and travelling on the Intercity up to London with me and your friend for your birthday treat.

You weren't supposed to get ill. You weren't supposed to know about suffering and pain. You should have been having fun without a care in the world. Not lying in a hospital bed with wires the whole spectrum of the rainbow hanging out of you.

It was a Saturday when it happened. You and Katie had come home after your gymnastics class. You always gave me a kiss on the cheek, but you didn't that day. You walked straight past me and up the stairs to your room. Katie must have seen the look on my face because she didn't follow you.

"She's not feeling right," she told me. "She couldn't even do a forward roll this morning. She kept saying her head hurt."

I knew it was serious. I just didn't want to believe it. I fetched some lemonade and *Jaffa Cakes* from the larder and put them on your favourite tray. The one with the mother and her kitten. I watched Katie's retreating back, listening to every tread on the stairs and the foot, edging your door open.

It was as if I had been waiting for the tray to crash to the floor. I found myself standing in your room as if no time had passed at all. You looked so peaceful laying there on the floor with your long hair framing your face. I looked at you then and I could see that beautiful woman you would one day grow into. But you weren't going to, were you, Jenny? You were going to be taken away from me. I knew that straight away.

Katie screamed. I had forgotten she was even there. She couldn't stop screaming and I found myself joining her. The paramedics found us like that, with our arms round one another, rocking back and forth. I always thought I was strong. I thought I could get through anything. But it's different with a child. You were my world, Jenny.

It took me a while to understand what the doctors were saying. "She's had a brain haemorrhage…"

But children didn't have brain haemorrhages, not just like that. The doctor was so kind; he hated telling me that, sadly, children did. They operated on you, but it didn't look good. He thought I should prepare myself for the worst. He said it wouldn't be long before you slipped away, that it would be for the best as the extent of damage to the brain would be devastating. I went blank after that.

I couldn't think, speak, move or function in any way. I didn't want to, either. I wanted to die, too. I didn't want to wake up and know you weren't going to be there any more. But how could I do that? You needed me. You needed your mum.

I made myself go and see you. You looked lost in

that huge hospital bed, with your head covered in bandages. I stood there for a long time. I couldn't believe it. Not my little girl. I kept expecting you to open your eyes and smile. I wanted you to sit up and talk to me, ripping the tubes and yanking the bandages from your head. I wanted you to tell me it was all a mistake. But you weren't going to do that, were you, Jenny?

I stayed with you all night and the next and the one after that. I didn't care about anything else, only being there with you. I talked to you so much during those long days: I told you how much I loved you and how I would always be there for you; I talked about daft things, too, and made up silly stories like I used to when you were small. Stories about fairies and princesses.

I even made up a story about a special daffodil. It was Mrs Farmer's biggest one. I pretended to pick it and wave it over your head like the magic wand you used to wave over me whenever I felt poorly. Shimmering stars floated down from the daffodil, falling onto your head, working their medicine as they made you better. I was sure I could see them, too. I think I had gone a little bit mad then.

I wanted to fill your room with daffodils, but they wouldn't let me. "No flowers. It's hospital policy," the staff nurse told me.

So I held your hand instead and I looked round that room and imagined it was covered from floor to ceiling with daffodils. I told you about each and every one of them and just when I thought I really had lost it, the doctor came. I knew it was time.

I cried so much that day, just like I am crying now.

I put the daffodil back in the vase, so very carefully. I smile through my tears and think of you.

A hand touches my shoulder. I reach up and grip it tightly.

"Why are you crying?"

I turn round and look at you. The scars are still there, but you are so beautiful. I close my eyes, still unable to believe the doctor's words that day.

"We ran some tests this morning and we're astounded by her progress. I wouldn't be surprised if she wakes up in the next day or so. They'll be more operations and I'm afraid I can't guarantee what's going to happen, but there's hope."

I open my eyes and I can't believe you are still here, returned to me today. I can't speak, but I don't need to, do I, Jenny?

"You put daffodils in my room, Mum. There's vases of them everywhere," you say and smile. "They're so pretty. Can I hold one?"

I smile, too, and take a daffodil from the vase. I place it in your hands. "Of course you can," I say.

BLUE-EYED BOY

He paused, feeling the dampness of leaves and sharp twigs poking at his tangled coat. His green eyes, huge and bright, cut through the blackness of the night.

He looked in through the glass door, his heart aching as the flames crackled and danced, a ball of orange reaching out to warm him. But it wasn't his house; it wasn't his family crowded round the fire. He watched faces spread into smiles and hands touch. A mum and dad, sitting in armchairs, were laughing over something, heads tipping back as chuckles filled the air. Close by, a boy and girl were sitting on the floor, playing some kind of game. He closed his eyes, imaging himself on a lap, snuggling right in, a hand gently stroking his fur. A purr would build, until his engines were at full steam. Or perhaps he'd invade the gameboard, push the counters out of place. The children would be annoyed, for a moment, before they'd giggle and arms would be around him – their beloved boy.

A cobweb tugged on his whiskers and his nose twitched, smelling the intruder. His eyes flew open. He spotted the legs, long and lean, battling to get away. He was faster; he had to be. Food had been scarce that day.

A movement caught his eye. He was drawn back inside. For a moment, he stared at his own reflection before realisation dawned. Another feline, fatter, plump even, was staring back at him. Her nose in the air, she turned away, the light bouncing off her gleaming coat. Jealousy invaded his body as the young girl crouched beside the cat. Her hands reached out to pet her lovingly. He watched as the cat writhed, delighting in the touch of her mistress. His eyes sad, he looked up at the girl.

She froze, catching sight of him. The distaste apparent, she called to her family. "Mum! Dad! There's a horrible cat outside. Its coat looks all mangled and scabby. Yuck! Make it go away."

"Shoo! Off you go," a hand banged the glass. "Filthy creature. Probably carrying all sorts of diseases. Go on. Get out of it!" the father snarled.

The mother joined in, their shouts filling the air and hatred glaring in their eyes.

He turned and ran on, his paws scrabbling for purchase as a door creaked open. Splash! A trickle of water tickled his fur. At least he'd missed the worst of it. His legs carried him out into the street. He'd not gone far before he noticed his stomach was hurting and the open wounds on his back stinging, reminding him of his recent brush with death. He closed his eyes, not wanting to see the monster again, huge and ugly, not wanting to hear its fierce roar, the beast bearing down upon him, the beep blaring in his ear.

The safe sanctuary of the bushes welcomed him, their muskiness a soothing scent. He sank down, his fur squelching on the musty leaves. Tiredness fell upon him and he was soon lost in the innocence of sleep. A smile played at the corners of his mouth, the dream already beginning.

"Archie! Archie!" the blue-eyed boy called.

Relishing the feel of the boy's hands, he arched his back and purred furiously, not wanting it to end.

He had been so excited, knowing the stack of boxes and empty rooms meant something new. Suddenly, he had panicked, watching his bowls and treats being packed away. The boy, his beloved master, had reassured him, telling him tales of the beautiful countryside they were moving to. "There's the most enormous garden, with trees, and Dad's going to build me a treehouse. Just think of the adventures we can have!"

But it had all gone wrong. Somehow, he had been left behind. He had waited, so sure they would come back. A week had passed, then two more. He had gone to find them, but now he didn't know where he was.

His breathing deepened and he allowed himself to become lost, lost in a world where he was safe and loved. A world where there was no one else, just him and his blue-eyed boy.

**

He knew he shouldn't have taken the food, but he was so hungry.

"Come on, young sir," a woman's voice said, picking up the contraption he'd found himself trapped in. She sounded kind and he could tell she was trying not to swing him too vigorously from side to side.

It was the monster! He pushed himself as far down as he could go as doors opened and slammed shut and he found himself inside the beast. But it wasn't for long.

He didn't know where the woman had taken him,

nor what she was going to do with him, but she had a strange machine she was holding over him. Bleep!

"Yes!" she said, smiling at him and caressing the top of his head gently.

She took him to a funny little room. There was a bed in there, some toys and best of all – food, which he gobbled down in seconds. A wave of tiredness swept over him and he settled down in the soft, warm bed.

"Archie! Archie!" his blue-eyed boy called.

He knew he was dreaming again, but something was wrong. Suddenly, there were arms around him and tears trickling onto his fur.

"Archie! We've found you!" his blue-eyed boy cried.

And, this time, he knew he wasn't dreaming.

THE DIARY OF ELLIE CARTER, AGED 6 ¾

<u>Monday 10th May</u>

I hate Phoebe Spencer-Rowbotham. She talks like the Queen and she thinks she's the best at everything. But she isn't. And she smells, too.

<u>Tuesday 11th May</u>

I really hate Phoebe Spencer-Rowbotham. I had to sit next to her on the carpet for stories and she kept poking me. It really hurt. I didn't want to squeal, but Phoebe made me. Then Miss Cook told me off. It's not fair.

<u>Wednesday 12th May</u>

Phoebe Spencer-Rowbotham is horrid. She told Miss Cook that I poked my tongue out at her when Miss Cook was looking the other way. I didn't. But I poked it out at Phoebe. And I'm going to do it again tomorrow.

<u>Thursday 13th May</u>

Phoebe Spencer-Rowbotham is a big pile of poo. She

has been telling everyone about her birthday party. She's going up to London and they're going to go everywhere and see everything. I've never been to London. It's not fair.

Friday 14th May

I really like Phoebe Spencer-Rowbotham. She gave me an invitation to her birthday party today.

LOVE LOST

Tears stung Beth's eyes as she walked along the beach. The harsh wind blew against her face, her nose streaming and cheeks smarting. She stared at the black clouds looming, full of rain and waiting to burst open. Her beautiful Labrador puppy was surging ahead, panting with excitement. A smile crept onto her face as he looked round at his mistress, wagging his tail merrily.

She reached her usual secluded area of beach and sank down into the sand. She always went there when she felt unhappy and lately, she had been visiting the spot more and more.

Beth watched the small dog dart into the sea, sploshing and splashing around. Strider; she'd named him aptly. He always had to take his dip in the sea, even when the water was freezing, but he soon hurried back to her, shaking icy cold water over her in the process. Still, she didn't care; she loved him. He was all she had left now.

Her thoughts drifted back as she listened to the waves crashing against the rocks nearby. A tall, handsome man came into her mind, intruding upon her thoughts. She remembered laughing and joking with him as they'd run through the waves, hand in hand, the summer sun shimmering down.

A tear rolled down her cheek as she recollected his words of love to her. He'd said their love was forever, that he would never leave her. He'd lied. She buried her face in her hands, the tears flowing freely.

A wet tongue rudely interrupted her. She looked into the pup's eyes. His brown ones gazed up at her, a look of concern on his face. She smiled through her tears and hugged him close.

Beth felt another's eyes on her and whirled round. But no one was paying her any attention. She watched as people strolled along the beach. It was late November and they still came. She looked at the mother with her children, trying to keep them under control while they surged towards the sea for a paddle in their wellingtons.

She smiled, noticing an elderly couple gazing tenderly at each other, oblivious to anything but their love for one another.

Her eyes became fixed on a figure a little further down the beach. The boy was throwing pebbles into the sea. Beth studied his face; such sadness reflected there. She frowned at his paleness and his eyes, dull and lifeless, with black rings circling them.

He turned in her direction. Beth looked down, feeling embarrassed at her stare. Minutes passed. She looked back. He was standing right by her. She blushed, smiling up at him.

"Hello," he said. "Can I stroke your dog? I love dogs, but Mummy is allergic to them so we can't have one."

"Of course you can," Beth said. "Your poor mummy. Do dogs make her sneeze?"

"Yes, and her eyes water, too. Mummy's dead now. I'm going to die like Mummy did. It's the cancer."

Beth couldn't speak. Her eyes filled with tears. "I'm so sorry," she whispered.

"It's okay, I'm not scared of dying. I'm going to be with Mummy again. But I don't want to leave Daddy. He'll be so lonely without us."

The tears came; she couldn't help it. She looked at the boy. He should have his whole life before him. She thought of his mother and felt her pain. And the father, to lose a wife and then cruellest of all – a child.

"Please don't be sad," the young boy reached out and held her hand. "Everything will be all right."

"Jacob! Jacob!" Shouts filled the air.

"That's my dad. I've got to go now." He let go of her hand and turned away. The small legs pumped up and down as he ran to his father.

Beth looked down at her hand, a tingling sensation shooting through her. Her eyes came up and found the boy's father, taking in his haggard and worn face. Beth turned away from them and marched in the other direction, her mind alive.

The next day dawned brighter than the last. Beth and Strider made their way to the beach. Beth looked at the puppy clasped to her chest, almost an exact replica of Strider. She stroked the furry animal, wondering why she was making such a fuss of a toy. Hopefully Jacob would like him.

An hour passed and still there was no sign of Jacob. Beth sighed. Why should there be? Why would he come to the beach again? She'd never seen him there before.

The clouds scuttled across the sky, shading the sun. Huge drops of rain splattered down to merge with the sea. Beth pulled her hood down over her head and called for Strider. It was time to go home.

Then she saw him. Jacob's father was standing by the path, staring out to sea. He looked so sorrowful and he was all alone. Beth swallowed the lump in her throat; something had happened. She squeezed the little dog in her palm, knowing Jacob would never set eyes on him.

She took a step forward and another until she was right beside Jacob's father. She knew she shouldn't ask…

"Excuse me. Is Jacob okay?" Her voice came out as a croak. "I saw him yesterday and…" She stopped, watching as he stared at her as if she were the strangest being on Earth.

"Jacob died two years ago."

"I'm so sorry. So sorry." Beth's hands flew to her mouth and she stumbled away.

"Hey, you dropped this," he said, picking up the cuddly toy. "Jacob would have loved this. He loved dogs. Did you see him here? The beach was his favourite place."

Beth turned to face him. "Yes, I saw him here. He was a lovely boy."

"Yes, he was." Beth thought she saw a lone tear trickle down his cheek. "Look, we're getting wet. Would you like a coffee? The café's open. Perhaps you can tell me about when you saw Jacob. I'm Richard, by the way."

"Beth." She smiled, not knowing what had happened the day before, but somehow it didn't matter any more.

***

Neither noticed a small figure watching over them. The little boy smiled. Everything was going to be all right.

CREAM SCONES

Martin didn't need to look at a watch to know it was midday. It was just as well because he didn't have a watch and probably never would.
The park was so peaceful before the lunchtime rush. Today was no different. He could hear birds singing and children laughing as they begged their mothers to swing them higher and higher. Occasionally a bell would ring out to announce a bicycle passing through.
Though a lot of the time, it was just Martin – Martin and the park. He always spent his morning at the park and sat on his favourite bench. After a rough night, it was just the tonic he needed before facing a new day.
He would stare at the pond, watching the sunshine spread its bright rays across the water. Toddlers often came with bags of bread and bit chunks from the crusts before mothers fussed and ducks protested. But they were soon gone and Martin would find himself alone once more.
He breathed deeply, and closed his eyes, soaking up the sounds, feeling that despite everything that had gone on in his life, it was all worth living for.
And then it started, slowly at first. One or two passed by. He knew who they were – suits, businessmen, hurrying through the park to grab a quick sandwich before rushing back to important meetings and to make crucial calls. Like he had before everything went wrong.

He should hate them, but he didn't. It wasn't their fault he had lost everything. It wasn't his either. How was he to know his business partner would run off with everything and leave him with nothing? Still, that was all in the past now.

Opening his eyes, he knew what would come next. He was right. Dirty looks. Upturned noses. It was time to move on.

He carried on through the park, watching benches fill and the daring business folk brave the slightly damp grass. In summer, the grass would be bursting with colour – oranges, reds, whites, yellows and, of course, the serious ones who always wore black, with just a hint of humanity in their stark white shirts and jokey ties.

A smile started to spread as he reached the old bandstand. It was almost time now. Surely. Papers were packed away and empty packets placed in bins. Almost time for the second wave.

His eyes lit up as they feasted on a discarded bacon butty being tossed into one of the bins nearby. It was probably from 'Ma's Kitchen' round the corner. Martin loved her ham rolls made with the most tender meat and bread, spread with thick butter. Not many ham rolls were left in the bin. It was always the burnt bacon butties. He knew he shouldn't be fussy, but he always had been, especially since Mary had come along.

At least he thought she was called Mary or should be. It suited her. Mary, with her golden hair and deep brown eyes. Well, he thought they were brown, but he had never been close enough to check.

She always had her lunch at one. She would arrive

at the park about five past and sit on the bench in front of the bandstand. Without fail, she looked up at the bandstand every time. Her eyes took on such a sad look he wanted to run up to her and take her in his arms, to tell her everything was all right.

But he didn't. He never would. He didn't want to see the loathing in her eyes when she looked at him. And there would be loathing. How could there not be? He wasn't much to look at, especially not now with his third-hand coat and worn trousers the colour of dirty canal water. He knew he needed a shave – a very long shave.

No, Mary would hate him and he couldn't bear that. Better to let the dream live on. And the cream scones. Martin smiled. She would be here at any moment. He ducked behind a bush.

She only used to bring one scone. The first time he had seen her, she had nibbled round the sides and thrown the rest away. Martin couldn't believe his luck. He had always been a sucker for scones.

As soon as Mary had gone, he had launched himself at the bin, stuck his hand in and emerged triumphant. The cigarette butt taking centre stage in the middle of the cream had ruined things a little. After one bite, he forgot all about it.

Ever since, she had brought two scones. She daintily nibbled upon one as before and then picked the other one up. She would smile as she looked at it before placing them both carefully in the rubbish bin.

It had puzzled Martin at first. He wondered if it were some silly diet thing that women seemed to get obsessed about. And then he didn't care any more. A scone was a scone.

Martin hoped she didn't stop coming. As he raised his head over the top of the bush to glimpse the first glint of gold, he knew it wouldn't be the scones he missed the most.

***

Sally turned the corner and there was the bandstand right before her. She smiled. David, as she had named him, was there behind the bush as usual.

She sat down and looked up at the once ornate bandstand, and sighed. Her dad had played here many years ago. Twenty years to be precise. He had been brilliant on his trombone. Sally remembered watching him on a scorching hot summer's day. She and Mum had been so proud of him. And then he had died, claimed by cancer.

Sally tore her eyes away and reached into her bag. Two scones. She picked one out and ate around the edges. Delicious, heavenly, even on a daily basis.

She patted her slim stomach. She oughtn't to be eating them at all, shouldn't even have been on that first day, but after seeing the ecstasy on David's face as he licked the cream from his lips, she knew she had to do it again.

As she took a last bite, she thought about him. David. She had known him for three months now. Three months of cream scones.

She had been shocked to see him rummaging through the bin and surface with her half-eaten scone. She had wanted to turn away but shame made her stay and watch. Shame that her initial instinct was to be as far away from him as possible.

He was young, about her age – too young to live like this. He was handsome, too, underneath the dirt and beard. She didn't like beards, but there was something about his, something about him.

Sally smiled. She put her scone back in the box along with the untouched one and gently lowered it into the bin. Time to go.

She walked away, feeling his eyes on her. She passed the bush, so close and yet not close enough. Walking on, she listened to feet shuffle and wrappers rustle.

Then she stopped and turned, just like she always did. She usually turned back and went on her way to work. This time she didn't. She moved further forward, right where he could see her if he just looked her way. Maybe that was what she wanted.

***

Martin grinned. Mary had looked even more beautiful today. Perhaps it was the sunny weather. Perhaps he was in love. He bit down on the scone, squirting jam onto his coat. In love, indeed. But he was. He knew it. A love that could never be.

***

Sally smiled. He had jam everywhere – over his coat, over his fingers and around his mouth. She fought the urge to go to him and trace her finger over his lips, to let the jam ooze onto her finger.

Her smile faded. He would probably scream if she did that or run away and she wouldn't see him again.

But what if he didn't?
Something surged inside her. She was going to talk to him. She took a step forward. And stopped. She took another step. If she didn't do it today, she never would. Besides, he had seen her now and it would be a shame to miss such an opportunity on such a glorious day.

***

Martin's mouth dropped open. Mary was walking towards him. She was smiling at him. She was close now. So close. He let the remainder of his scone drop back into the bin. Suddenly, there was something more important than scones on his mind.
She was right beside him now. He looked into those deep brown eyes.
"Hello, I'm Sally."
"I'm Martin. It's good to meet you, Sally."

***

Sally smiled. It was a good job she had done some overtime recently; it looked like she would be taking the afternoon off.

A CHILD'S DREAM

I hate it here. I huddle under the covers, pulling them over my head. Big drops of sweat ooze out of my skin, even though it's cold. Slowly, I start to rock to and fro. Mummy said I did that when I was a baby, with my bottom stuck up in the air, my thumb in my mouth and the other hand twiddled amongst the knots in my long hair.

I begin to drift away to find peace, my safe place to escape to, to save me from my horrible life. The three of us are sitting under the tree: Mummy, Daddy and me. Daddy smiles at us, the bright yellow sun shining down on his blue eyes making them twinkle like the stars. He starts his story, tales of pixies, elves and fairies. My eyes light up, my imagination running riot. Mummy opens up the picnic basket and I see the treats inside. Chocolate. Bars and bars of chocolate.

Mummy turns to look at me. Her face has changed: her yellow eyes flash, her nose is hooked and her mouth twists into a sneer. I get up and run to Daddy. Daddy will save me. He holds his arms out, long and bendy like pieces of toffee candy. He grabs me and laughs, a vampire moving in for the kill.

My legs are sprinting, my arms flapping, my head spinning. Footsteps pound after me, not letting go of their prize. I dare to look behind. Nothing. They have gone. Mummy and Daddy have abandoned me.

I awake to find sunlight soaking up the room. It's bouncing off the sunflower walls. I hate yellow. I like pink. The walls of my bedroom at home are pink. I shiver, my daydream returning. It has been the same for a long time, but the ending has changed over the past week. I used to love that happy place. Just Mummy, Daddy and me. The three of us would stay there for hours under our tree, telling stories and eating chocolate. But not any more. Mummy and Daddy aren't nice now. They wouldn't have left me if they were nice.

Wetness soaks my pillow. I am crying. "Mummy! Daddy! I don't mean it. You are nice. Mummy! Daddy!" my voice is getting louder.

I can't stop it. My body is shaking and the howls filling the room are coming from my mouth. I want my mummy. I want my daddy.

"There, there, pet. It's all right."

Arms are around me. A gentle pat on the head. I look up, full of hope. But it's not them. It's Mandy.

"Oh, Alice. I'm so sorry," Mandy says to me.

"I want my mummy. Where's Daddy? Is he coming to get me later?"

"No, pet. I wish they were both here. I wish I could bring them back."

"Is it nice in heaven? Daddy said God looks after everybody in heaven. He said everyone plays and runs and there's always lots to eat."

"That's right. They'll be happy there. They can look down on you at any time and see what you're doing. They'll always be with you. Here. In your heart." Mandy smiles, her own tears spilling onto my bed. "Your grandma's coming to see you today."

My arms stiffen and my breathing is loud inside my ears. Granny Hampshire, my daddy's mummy. I only liked Granny and Grampy Brown, but they went up to heaven two years ago. There's only Granny Hampshire left now.

The Dragon, Mummy called her, though her skin is more white than green. But her eyes are green. Green like a toad, not the nice green on trees. She looks like a witch I've seen on TV, with warts all over her skin and long, pointed nails. Granny Hampshire always wears black. Daddy said that's because she is still in mourning over Grampy Hampshire's death. I've never seen him except in pictures. I think he died a hundred years ago or something like that. He looks very stern in all his photos. I don't think I would have liked him and I don't like Granny Hampshire either. I've only seen her three times. Well, Mummy says I saw her lots when I was a baby because we lived with her for a while. Mummy says they had no choice and she said it was the last place on Earth they wanted to go, but they had to think of me. I don't remember it. I'm quite glad because Mummy said it was like staying in a prison camp, whatever that is. It doesn't sound like a nice place anyway.

Mandy says Granny is coming to see me after the funeral. She says I'm too young to go. I would like to say goodbye to Mummy and Daddy. But if they are already in heaven, I don't know how I can. So I'm going to stay here with Mandy.

I like Mandy. She isn't very pretty and she's quite large. Plump, Mummy would say. More to cuddle. I don't like anyone else here. The children all smell funny, like they wet the bed. I had to share a room with a girl called Lucy. She always wet the bed. Lucy has gone now, to a foster home, Mandy said.

I wish I was going to a foster home, instead of living with Granny Hampshire. I wish I had someone to love me like Lucy. A nice new mummy and daddy, who would read me a story at night and let me have milk and a biscuit before bed and give me lots of cuddles. Mummy and Daddy did that, except the biscuit bit.

The day of the funeral is here. I stare out the window, the rain beating out a tune on the glass. Two figures are on the path. They look up and wave at me frantically. I race down the stairs, almost tripping over my huge teddy bear slippers. I pull the door open, a smile on my face and my heart clapping like thunder. Mummy! Daddy! My arms are wide open. I stop. And scream. And fall to the ground. There is no one there. They have gone. I won't ever see them again.

"What on earth is she doing?" a nasty voice in my ear.

Hands grab me, yanking me to my feet. My eyes bleary and wet, I look into her face.

The witch is here. Her black cloak wraps around me. Her lips are red like the wine Daddy used to drink. She is going to eat me whole. Her huge, black teeth widen to show the gigantic, black cave inside.

I tremble, unable to save myself. I give in. Maybe the end will be quick. Maybe Mummy and Daddy will take me away with them. We can all be together again. A family once more. I screw my eyes tightly shut. I wait for the pain. I know she will eat me. I've read books and seen pictures. I know what they can do to children.

A kiss. I'm sure I heard a kiss and something soft touched my cheek. I dare to open my eyes. She strokes my face. I'm sure she is crying. It must be the rain.

"Come along then. Time to go home," she says and takes my hand.

I sit in the black car watching the unfamiliar streets. She lied. We are not going home. I swallow, a big lump stuck in my throat. I won't cry. I mustn't let her see me cry. Witches don't like children who cry. They laugh at them and call them silly names before they eat them.

"You're quiet, girl," her voice is like the sudden bang of a bursting balloon.

"I'm okay."

"Speak up. I can't hear you. And what did that awful woman give you?"

"Mandy's not awful. She gave me a teddy bear. She's really, really nice. I want to stay with Mandy!"

"The youth of today. No manners. We'll soon sort you out, my girl. And you won't be seeing Amanda again, of that, I can assure you."

The trip drags on forever. Day has changed into night. Traffic lights blind me, the rain making the red light shimmer. I fumble for the lock, pulling it up. I open the door, battling with my seat belt. The gnarled hand grabs me, jagged nails digging into my arm.

"Close the door. Now!" her thunder roars.

I do as she says. I have no choice.

Our final destination is in sight. The driveway is long and twisted. I see it: her mansion, dark and grey. The windows are barred and I know every single one will have a lock.

I slowly get out the car, my eyes busily searching the grounds. Trees. There are trees everywhere. I can't remember when I last saw another house or person. My legs want to run, but there is nowhere to run to.

Branches bend towards me, arms reaching out to take me. I run to the door, the same pale grey as Granny's hair.

"In you go then, girl. We haven't got all day. It's dark and I've supper to prepare."

My head says no, but my feet take me forward. We are in the hall and a light the yellow of Mummy's custard shines down. All I can see are paintings. Huge, ugly paintings of hideous people. Witches. They all look like witches.

"They're your ancestors, Alice. Now, I'll show you to your room and then you can help with supper."

I follow Granny, my arm on the banister as we weave round and round the never-ending staircase. The walls seem to close in on me, monstrous shadows dancing on the chipped, grey paint.

I'm at the top and my scream is out. My eyes stare into those of the knight.

"Don't be so silly, Alice, it's only a suit of armour. Goodness me, you've got a lot of growing up to do, haven't you? At your age, I was out working."

"I'm only ten."

"I thought you were twelve. Still, you'll learn a thing or two while you're here."

She turns a handle and a door opens. I walk in and I can't stop crying.

"What's wrong now? This is a lovely room."

I stare at the iron bed and bright, white sheet. A bookcase stands in the corner, empty like the wardrobe towering above me. A chest of drawers completes the room, rows of dolls sitting stiffly on it. Their eyes are small, vacant black holes. I'm sure I saw one wink at me. The hairs on the back of my neck are standing upright and my skin is clammy.

"Don't you like the dolls? They're my special collection. I've put them in here to make you feel at home," Granny says, a hand on my shoulder. "I'll give you five minutes to unpack your case and then I'll be back for you. Would you like to peel the potatoes or prepare the cabbage?"

"I don't want any supper. I want to go home," my voice gets smaller.

"This is your home now, Alice. Look, just for tonight you can forgo supper. But from tomorrow, things are going to be very, very different. You need to learn a few manners, my girl."

I sit down on the hard mattress, alone with no one to love me. I take Mandy's teddy from my case and put it next to my pillow. Maybe teddy will love me. I lay my head on the lumpy pillow, surprised when my eyelids begin to droop.

And I'm back there with Mummy and Daddy under our special tree. But something isn't right. Someone else is here. It's her. The witch. Her hair is tight in a bun and her wrinkled face is full of anger. She is ten feet tall as she is coming for me.

"Mummy! Daddy! Save me. Please. Please come back. Mummy! Daddy! Where are you?"

"I'm here. I'm here. It's all right, Alice."

Someone strokes my hair and kisses my head. My

eyes open to see Mummy. She has come back. Her smooth skin wriggles and lines cover her face. The long, blonde hair turns grey and the singsong voice is croaky and rasping. Granny has come for me.

"Oh, Alice. I know, I know. There, there. It'll be all right. I'll look after you."

The hands are surprisingly soft and soothing. I allow myself to be held, almost feeling comforted.

"I'll stay with you tonight, Alice. Just this once. Yes. It won't hurt just this once."

Granny climbs into bed, the skin on her arms cold and leathery against my sweaty ones.

The sun peeps round a corner of the thick curtain. I didn't think I would sleep. Maybe Granny cast a spell. Her snoring is loud in my ear and her arms stiff around me. I feel her hair, silky against my cheek. She splutters awake, her body jerking and pulling away from me.

"What the he – Oh yes, I remember." She reaches for the lamp and we blink at each other. "Chop, chop then. Time to get up."

Our heads swing round, shock on our faces as the door opens. A shadow enters the room. My hands fly to my mouth. A witch's cat, black and evil, jumps on the bed.

"Hello, Harry. Come and meet Alice. She'll be staying with us from now on and I want you to take special care of her. This is to be your sleeping place, Harry. I certainly can't stay here every night. No, that really wouldn't do," Granny is stern.

The creature edges closer and breaks into a noisy purr. My hands can't help but reach out to stroke him. Harry's green eyes flash and a look of complete bliss covers his whole face. At last, I have found a friend.

"Right, Harry. Off you go. Go and see Grampy," Granny says. "We've got to get on."

Goosebumps spread over my skin. Suddenly, I'm very, very cold.

"Don't look at me like that. Alice, stop being so silly. Grampy's Harry's brother. He's not as nice as Harry. He's got a bit of a nasty streak in him, but you'll be all right."

I collapse back on the bed. I'm not sure I can take much more.

"Can I have a bath?" That always makes me feel better.

"A bath? On a Wednesday morning? Sunday night is bath night. I'll give you five minutes to get dressed. After that it's breakfast and on to lessons."

"You mean I can go to school?" I hardly dare hope.

"Don't be absurd. I'm going to take care of your schooling. Then it's chores this afternoon."

"But I want to go to school."

"Alice, you must stop questioning my judgement. I will not have it."

She is gone. I'm sure in a puff of smoke. A tear rolls down my cheek. I'm a prisoner, stuck here forever and ever. I brush my hair, staring at the tangles in the mirror I discovered nesting among the dolls. A face joins me in the glass. I twist round. Nothing. I look back. Daddy. He grins at me and winks before vanishing.

"Come back, Daddy. Please. I don't like it here. I want my daddy!"

"It's all right," a breath of wind, an echo.

I'm sure it was him. I'm sure I heard Daddy. I smile into the mirror. Daddy is with me.

I venture down the stairs and along the corridor. I run past the suit of armour. I'm certain he moved his arm. I pause on the staircase, my eyes catching sight of the huge spider creeping towards me. Its hairy legs are black and the length of a ruler and its eyes are beady, jutting out from its generous body. I'm going to die.

"There you are, Horace. He's taken a liking to you, Alice." Granny scoops him up and disappears from view.

No one can move that quickly, especially when they are as old as she is. My hands unglue themselves from the banister and my feet find feeling. I make it down the stairs in one piece and I eventually find the kitchen. An enormous cauldron is taking up most of the room. I'm sure I heard a frog croak from inside. Rows and rows of jars line the walls of iron racks. I scan the labels, searching for potions.

"I see you're admiring my spices. I do like cooking." Granny enters the room and walks over to stir the bubbling liquid in the cauldron. "Do you like porridge?"

"Yes," my voice is small, my mind imagining all the horrid ingredients Granny has put in the porridge.

She leads me into the dining room and my eyes take in the huge banquet hall. I'm sure that's what they call it in the history books. The walls are covered with beasts, their eyes bulging and horns ready to lunge at someone. I picture Granny, her hair flowing out behind her, the enormous weapon in her hand. She is running, faster than the stag ahead. She launches the spear. It flies through the air. I shudder. I can't follow it through.

"Your place is here." Granny points to my seat.

I struggle to pull out the wooden chair, wondering if kings and queens sat on thrones like this.

"Mummy always lets me eat my breakfast in front of the telly." I don't know how the words came out.

Granny's face turns raspberry red and then purple like the veins in her legs. She turns to stare at the spear and then back to me. I gulp, wondering if I can make it to the front door in time.

Her face relaxes. "I know you youngsters like television, but I don't allow it in my house. Your father didn't know what one was until he left home. It never did him any harm to go without. Television is a dreadful modern-day invention."

Poor Daddy. I can see him, a small boy in grey shorts. He sits up to the table, his back straight and his hands in his lap. He bows his head and Granny says a prayer. He begins to eat, picking at his food with his hands. The cane smashes down on one hand. Shouts fill the air and he is sent to his room.

My daydream has gone and I'm sitting opposite Granny. Her eyes are closed and her hands clasped together. I do the same, hoping the cane is nowhere near.

"You may start." Her head jerks up and her eyes stare into mine.

I pick up a spoon and stir the cereal round and round.

"Not that spoon, Alice! Did your mother not teach you anything?"

The clatter of the spoon falling to the floor is like

the bang of cymbals in our music lesson at school. Granny's eyes are red, blinking into mine. I'm sure I'm going to die of fright. She looks down and continues with her food. I wonder if I'm free to go. My chair scrapes back and her glare tells me I'm not.

I've never seen anyone eat so quickly. There's definitely something very strange about Granny.

Before I realise it, I have been excused and we are upstairs. I'm sitting behind an old, wooden desk. I stare at the blackboard and white chalk. Granny taps the board and I cringe, imagining her long, yellow nails screeching down the surface.

A click hangs in the air. I turn to the door. I'm certain the key just turned. I look back to Granny over the other side of the room. She grins at me, before her mouth opens and a cackle is free. Her two black teeth hang down and I'm sure she's going to bite me.

"Right. We'll start with logarithms," she says.

"Log what? Why can't I go to school? I miss my friends. Sarah and me sat next to each other." My strength is gaining.

I can see the anger building inside her. She hates me. I know she does. I hate her, too. I can't look at her any more. My head hangs down, but if she hates me enough maybe she'll take me back to Mandy. Mandy will take care of me. Mandy loves me. She could be my new mummy. She would let me go to school with Sarah.

I can't stop crying. I don't want a new mummy. And I don't want to be here. I want my real mummy back. My tears splash down onto the wood. I stare at the deep marks in the grain. My daddy was here. His initials are clear in front of me. I finger them gently. I wonder if he was kept prisoner in this room like me. I can picture him, sitting here. A tiny boy, lost in the vast room. His tongue is out and he concentrates on his work, digging deeper into the wood. A shadow stands over him, looming closer and closer. Daddy looks up and screams. I can see fear on his face. He knows what is coming next. He is knocked from his seat and the shadow turns to face me.

The daydream has gone. But it wasn't Granny. Granny wasn't the monster. There is another in this house.

Granny wraps her arms around me and we rock back and forth. She kisses my hair and places her hand on top of mine. "Everything is going to be fine. It'll take time, but we'll be all right. Together. We'll get through it together."

I pull away. "Why are you crying, Granny?"

Granny wipes her tears. "Oh, Alice. Alice."

Now I'm the grown-up, hugging her close to me and telling her everything will be all right. I smell her hair. The sweet smell of strawberries surprises me. I can almost taste them and the lashings of cream Mummy always poured over them.

"It was Grampy, wasn't it? He was the monster, not you." I clasp my hands over my mouth, my mind finally remembering where I had seen his face before.

Granny nods, unable to speak. I can see him clearly now. A huge, hairy monster of a man. Granny tries to get into the room, but of course he has locked the door and pocketed the key. Granny outsmarts him, another in her pocket. She runs to her son's side.

She is too late and Daddy is on the floor. The monster turns to her and there is no stopping him.

I blink and stare at Granny. She looks up at me, red rings surrounding her eyes.

"I should have left him, Alice. We should have gone, me and my son. I should have saved my son. But he threatened to kill me if I did. Your daddy never forgave me for his childhood. I ruined it."

"You didn't. It wasn't your fault. Daddy knew that. I'm sure he did." I feel old beyond my years.

I look at Granny, the granny I don't really know. But I know she isn't a witch. She is a bit strange, but she isn't a witch.

"I just wish I could hold your daddy one more time."

"So do I. Mummy, too. But the nasty crash. That drunk man took them away from me." I am a child again.

We hold each other for a long time, each of us lost in our own thoughts.

Granny breaks the silence. "Let's forget lessons for today. It's such a nice morning, why don't we go and have a picnic lunch outside?"

My eyes are dry and I smile. A real smile for my granny. We hold hands and walk down the stairs. I look back and grin at the knight, poking my tongue out.

We enter the kitchen and my eyes light up at the goodies Granny takes from the cupboard. As we walk to the back door, we pass the cauldron. I'm sure she has swapped it for a normal cooking pot.

I feel warm sunshine on my face and the sound of birds singing fills the air. Granny laughs as she leads the way.

"I've dreamt of this moment for years, Alice. I never thought I would see this day. I hope you like it here. I am a bit old fashioned, but hopefully you'll not find me too bad underneath. I'm sure you will teach me a thing or two about the youth of today."

"I think it would help if you got a TV."

"Don't push your luck, young lady," Granny smiles.

My own smile has gone. I stand, sure my feet are being dragged into the ground.

Granny is spinning. I can see at least ten of her. The birds have changed into vultures and the sky is turning black. I focus my eyes and the tree looms closer.

It is the tree from my dream. It is everything I knew it would be; beautiful, green leaves and pink blossom reach out to me, a halo of light against the ugly scenery. I try to make it there safely, but Granny won't let me go. I will the tree to wrap its branches around me and to take me away. But I know it won't save me. My dream always turns into a nightmare.

"Alice. Alice, what's wrong?" Granny intrudes.

I break free from her and I am running. The tree sways, the pastel blossom waving to me. A few petals fall to the ground. My arms are outstretched, palms upwards, ready to catch the flowers.

Granny joins me, laughter in the air. She dances round and for some reason, I join her, a smile now on my face. We are covered in pretty pink. Granny's hand grabs mine and we can't stop giggling. Our feet seem to have minds of their own.

Granny falls to the ground and I'm dragged down

with her. Her breathing has stopped and her face is grey.

"Don't leave me. No! I love you, Granny!"

"Alice, I'm all right. I'm just not used to that sort of thing." Granny laughs, colour back in her face, her cheeks like a clown's.

She sits up and my hands are in the picnic basket, my stomach grumbling and wishing I had eaten breakfast.

"Alice, manners," a sternness is back in her voice.

I turn and look at Granny's finger wagging at me.

"I'm so sorry, Granny. I'll try and do better."

She smiles and we lay out the yummy sandwiches, sausage rolls and cake oozing with cream. I wait for Granny to say grace and I even use my napkin.

We tuck in and I look up at my special tree. I feel as if I'm dreaming. I am, because I'm sure I can see Daddy walking over to join us. He stops and looks round. Mummy is here, too. They hold hands and smile at me, each blowing me a kiss.

I blink. They have gone. I turn to Granny and she winks at me. I smile back, a wave of love gliding over me from head to toe. I'm going to like it here.

A NEW FRIEND

"Mum! Come and meet my new friend," Jake burst through the kitchen door.

Laura beamed at her son. "Your first day back at school went all right then?"

"It was okay, I suppose. But I've made a bestest ever new friend. Can he stay to dinner, Mum? Can he?"

"Well, if his mum knows where he is and she doesn't mind. It's sausages tonight. Does he like that?"

"Of course, Mum, it's his favourite."

Laura stared through the open door. "Where is he then?"

"He's right beside you, Mum. Do you like his smart red tie?"

Tears welled up in Laura's eyes. A habit since childhood, she tugged at her soft, blonde hair, her fingers tweaking the curls. "I'm sorry, Jake. Look, I'll get on with the dinner. It'll be another half an hour. Why don't you show your new friend your new toy car?"

Laura watched as Jake eagerly led the way, smiling at a friend only he could see. Once Jake had disappeared upstairs, Laura collapsed against the sink, sobs wracking every inch of her body.

"Oh, Tom, why did you have to leave us?" Her voice, a wail, filled the air.

She closed her eyes and Tom's handsome face was before her. Deep brown eyes crinkled as he smiled. His fingers flicked his fringe of chestnut hair from his face and his grin widened. Tom and Jake, like father, like son. Both were dark, so handsome and loving. Every day when her eyes fell on Jake, a fresh wave of hurt tore through her. Two months had passed since Tom's death, but the memory was still raw and ragged.

Her blue eyes slowly opened and Tom's countenance faded. She sighed, knowing she should be glad Jake was so happy, that he was beginning to rebuild his life. But he wasn't.

Not deep down. Why would he need an imaginary friend if everything was all right?

"Dinner's ready!" Laura called out a while later.

Footsteps thudded down the stairs and Jake's face appeared round the corner. "Great, we're starving. Mum, why have you set a place for Jasper?"

"Jasper?"

"Yes, it's a very nice name, isn't it? Anyway, Jasper doesn't sit at the table and he can't use a knife and fork. Don't you know anything about cats, Mum?"

"A cat? He's a cat? Yes, of course he's a cat," Laura said, a wave of sickness passing over her.

She had no choice but to go along with it and a bowl brimming with sausages was placed by the door for Jasper.

"See, Mum? He was very hungry," Jake said between mouthfuls.

Laura swung round and stared at the empty bowl. "But… how… you. I need to lie down."

She mounted the stairs, her knuckles white and gripping the stair rail. She opened the door to her bedroom and sank down onto the bed. Her eyelids closed and darkness took over.

Minutes, perhaps hours, passed. Laura awoke to a dull shroud hanging over the room. The half-moon shone a watery light on the bed, shadows dancing in the corner and shapes bouncing on the ceiling.

Tap, tap! She swivelled round at the knock on the door.

"There's someone to see you, Mum. Can I come in?" Jake's muffled voice asked.

"Yes, of course you can," Laura smiled, starting to feel a little better.

The door flew open and something black and furry sprang into the room and onto the bed.

"Jasper wanted to come and see you," Jake followed.

Laura studied the cat, green eyes staring back at her. "It's a cat, a real cat. And he's wearing a red bow tie," Laura said, goosebumps breaking out all over.

"Me and Jasper had a bit of a talk," Jake said.

"A talk? What's he doing now?" Laura backed away as the cat prodded her, moving closer and licking her hand with his tongue.

"He likes you. He wants you to stroke him. That's it. See, he's purring. Jasper wants to stay with us for a while. That's okay, isn't it?"

Laura couldn't speak. She was sure the cat had just winked at her.

"Daddy sent Jasper."

"Daddy?"

"Yes, Daddy thought we needed a friend. Jasper says Daddy's fine and being looked after. But Daddy thought I might need a bit of help, so he sent Jasper.

But Jasper and me agree you need a friend more. So I'm giving Jasper to you."

Laura stared at her son, so young and yet so wise beyond his years.

"It'll be all right, Mum. We'll be all right. The three of us."

Laura stroked the glossy coat, smiling as Jasper licked her again. He turned to her, his eyes boring into hers. Another wink. She had proof. But proof of what? She smiled. It didn't matter any more.

Somehow, she knew Jake was right. She was going to get through this. They all were.

FIRST SIGHT

The stench hit his nostrils. He was going to be sick, but it wasn't anything to do with the smell. Sweat oozed from his palms and he couldn't stop shaking. Shouts were gaining, a crowd chanting louder and louder. A roar pierced the air close by. The stale bread and filthy water he'd had for breakfast flew from his mouth. Hands grabbed him, jagged nails digging into flesh. Darkness, deeper and deeper, dragging him down. He smiled, snaking his way towards it. They wouldn't let him and yanked him to his feet, kicking him in the ribs, the back, the legs.

Sunlight stabbed him as he was hurled outside. A sea of eyes stared down at him, mocking, jeering, taunting. For a moment, he didn't care, unable to take his gaze from the magnificent sight. He hadn't believed them, but every word was true. It was the first time he had seen the Colosseum.

The lion pounced, ensuring it was his last.

MYSTERY MAYHEM

Matty knew he shouldn't have taken it. But it was such a brilliant thing, more brilliant in fact than anything he had ever seen in his entire life. Besides, he'd had no choice. His life wasn't worth living without it.

He stared at the object of his desire and licked his lips, running his hands over the smooth surface of the van. It had only been in his possession for ten minutes, but already it looked right at home in his bedroom amongst the *Scooby-Doo* wall stickers and matching duvet set.

Matty picked the *Mystery Machine* up and poked and prodded at its interior, marvelling at the fine craftsmanship. He smiled back at the grinning faces of *Shaggy* and *Scooby*. When the engine erupted into life and the lights flashed fiercely on and off, Matty's life was complete. Almost.

He sighed. It would have been better if the van was actually his and not Connor's next door. It was all his mum's fault really. She hated *Scooby-Doo*. She said her brother had forced her to watch it when she was little. She always said she couldn't stand 'those pesky kids'. He hated it when she said that. Grown-ups were all the same. They thought they were being so cool. They weren't. Matty thought she was talking a load of rubbish anyway. *Scooby-Doo* couldn't possibly be that old. Anyway, just because she didn't like it, it didn't mean he wasn't allowed to.

His dad stayed out of it. He had the right idea. His

mum seemed to change into a vile monster if anyone dared argue with her. Matty wouldn't have been surprised to see smoke flaring from her nostrils and her head rotate 360 degrees. No, he couldn't blame Dad, though Matty was sure he liked *Scooby-Doo* as much as Matty did; he'd caught his dad watching it enough times.

"I was flicking through the channels when I saw *Scooby* was on. I was just about to call you," Dad always said, smiling sweetly and then proceeding to give Matty an in-depth description of the last ten minutes of the show.

Matty knew his dad would like the *Mystery Machine*, too. After all, he was great at playing garages. And crashes. But whenever Matty asked Mum if he could have a *Mystery Machine,* she said no. And every time he asked his dad, Dad always told him to ask Mum, which brought it back to being his mum's fault. If she had let him have it when he had asked for it, he wouldn't have had to resort to stealing.

He gasped and almost dropped the van to the floor. Stealing. That was a terrible word. He hadn't stolen anything ever before. Well, not exactly. Some of the boys at school nicked chews from the corner shop. They had dared Matty to do it once.

He thought he would die from the amount of sweat soaking him from head to toe as he walked into the shop. His eyes had darted left. The aisle was empty. His eyes darted right. No one there either. His fingers shook as they reached out, closer and closer to their sugary prize. He scooped up a *Sherbet Fountain* and slid it into his coat pocket. Four options leapt into his mind – to faint, be sick, wet his pants or all three.

The *Sherbet Fountain* was placed perfectly back into its dusty slot before Matty sprinted from the shop. He didn't like *Sherbet Fountains* anyway.

Matty looked back at the van. He hadn't really stolen it, had he? The police took you away if you stole things. Everyone knew that. They put you in jail and fed you horrible food. Rats came and crawled over you in the night and spiders, too. It didn't smell very nice either. Matty didn't want to go to jail.

Suddenly, an idea ignited into his mind. He smiled. Everything was going to be all right because he had only borrowed it. But he hadn't borrowed it, had he? After all, now he had it in his grasp, he wasn't about to let it go again. No one knew how much he had yearned for the *Mystery Machine*. *Scooby-Doo* was the best ever TV programme in the world. Matty was his number one fan. And *Shaggy*'s, too. *Shaggy* always made him laugh. Matty knew all the baddies as well and everything about everyone in the show.

Mum had bought him a *Scooby-Doo* pyjama case, which was all right, as long as he remembered to shove it under the bed when his friends came round. She had tutted a lot when he had chosen his bedcovers and wall stickers, but she had let him have them – just not the *Mystery Machine*.

"What on earth do you want that hideous thing for?" she had said, winking at Dad and laughing.

Grown-ups were so unfair. No, he definitely hadn't borrowed it, especially when he thought about how the van came to be in his bedroom.

He always went round to Connor's house on a Saturday morning. Mum said it gave her a chance to 'catch up with things'. What things Matty had no idea, but she did the same for Connor's mum on a Sunday afternoon.

That Saturday morning had been like any other. They had been playing soldiers and Connor had just whacked Matty with his sword. Matty had swiftly swung his dagger into Connor's side and the fight was on. Plastic met plastic as they dived under the bed and leap-frogged over tables and toys.

"That's enough, you two. You'll come crashing through my ceiling in a minute," Connor's mum said, wagging her finger at them.

"I'm going to get a drink. Got any *Ribena*, Mum?" Connor said, making for the stairs.

"Get one for me," Matty yelled after him.

He felt Connor's mum's eyes on him.

"Please," he said.

She smiled and turned to follow her son. Matty scowled at her retreating back and then something caught his eye. He was sure he could see it – the *Mystery Machine* peeking out. It had been stuffed into a cardboard box and was almost hidden amongst colourful crayons, paperclips and scrappy bits of paper. Connor never took care of his toys. But why would he when he had everything?

Connor just had to look at a toy on the telly and it seemed to appear in his bedroom. He played with it all day long and then the next day it was thrown onto the floor to be forgotten along with all the other toys. Most of them ended up being broken. Cars were crushed and train tracks were trashed. Connor didn't care.

Matty had grabbed the *Mystery Machine*. Remarkably, it was still in one piece. He was surprised Connor hadn't shown it off to him before. He knew how much Matty wanted one. Connor had probably forgotten about it already. Matty couldn't bear to see it neglected or – even worse – stepped on and snapped like a mouldy old twig. He'd had to save it, hadn't he?

So he had slipped out there and then, his head bobbing up and down as he had peered round the banister and bolted for the door and freedom. No, that wasn't exactly borrowing.

Matty twirled his fingers round a clump of hair, yanking madly as a finger became stuck. He could almost hear his mother's words: "He always does that when he's feeling guilty about something."

But he wasn't. He didn't feel guilty at all. Matty chewed his lip. Even if he did, he couldn't do anything about it, could he? Or perhaps he could. Connor wouldn't even notice it was gone. Matty was sure he could creep back there now. He could make up an excuse, say his mum had called him home for something. Matty grinned. His plan was foolproof.

He threw open his bedroom door, jumped down the stairs two at a time and opened the front door. He took a step forward – and stopped.

The most awful shrieking sound blasted into his ears. Matty's heart sank. It was coming from next door.

"My… my… my van's gone. He… he… he took it," Connor's wailing grew to a crescendo.

Matty quickly closed the front door. What was he

going to do? Things couldn't get any worse now.

"Matty, what are you doing? I thought you were next door. What's that you've got in your hands?"

"Nothing." Matty's hands flew behind his back.

He gulped and felt very sick as his mother strode towards him.

"If it's nothing, you won't mind showing me your hands then, will you?"

One hand opened. Then the other. Matty tried to look surprised to find the *Mystery Machine* in his hands, but one look at his mother's face and he knew she wasn't having any of it.

"How dare you look through my wardrobe? I thought I could trust you, Matty. I knew you wanted the van and I thought it would be a special surprise for your birthday. Couldn't you wait just one more week? You've ruined everything now," she said, sobbing.

Matty sighed. It looked like it was time for the truth. His shoulders slumped. Though, perhaps it wasn't so bad. In a week's time, he would have his very own *Mystery Machine*. That is, if his mum ever forgave him.

One thing was certain: his days as a thief were definitely over. Besides, he had been going to give it back all along, hadn't he?

IN SEARCH OF DINOSAURS

"What's he doing now?" Cliff frowned, his hand gripping the tea towel.

He turned to his wife and she joined him at the sink. Sighing, they stared out the window.

"It's all your dad's fault. I told you not to let Jack spend too much time with him, but you wouldn't listen. Jack is just like him," Mary said.

Cliff ground his teeth together. "My father was a good man. Anyway, Jack's nothing like him."

He looked over at the object of discussion. Jack was small for his age and often mistaken for a five-year-old, instead of the eight years he had lived on Earth. His soft blond hair was swaying in the breeze as his shiny sea-green eyes focused on the task in hand.

"He's going to be just like your father. Your father was nutty as a fruitcake. I can see it now," Mary said, folding her arms. "Look at him. He thinks he's a mole. He's ruining my garden. I'm going to put a stop to this."

***

Jack smiled at his companion, George. The iguana never left his side.

"They're here somewhere, George. I'm about to make the discovery of the year. Hoorah!" Jack said, extracting a worm from the ground. "Yes, it's a descendant of the great Wormasaurus. They roamed the Earth…"

"Jack! Get inside now. You're covered in mud and you've pulled up my Buddleia," his mum stalked towards him and grabbed his arm. "Up to your room."

"You're treading on George. Don't hurt him, Mum."

"It's a plastic toy, for goodness' sake, Jack."

Jack blinked back the tears and broke free from her. He pounded up the stairs and into his bedroom, slamming the door behind him. He slumped onto his bed, willing his body to mould into the sheets.

As he gave in to tears, he felt huge, glinting eyes staring straight down at him. Tyrannosaurus Rex, Deinonychus, his favourite Diplodocus, Stegosaurus, Brachiosaurus and Parasaurolophus all looked at him from the posters covering the walls.

Jack's vision blurred and the beasts all rolled into one. He turned over and rocked himself back and forth. He longed for sleep, for a beautiful dream to take over. In his dreams he was safe. Grandpa always came to him in his dreams. He missed Grandpa. His mum said he'd had a heart attack. Grandpa was only fifty-five. His mum said that wasn't very old. Jack thought it was ancient, though not as ancient as the dinosaurs.

Jack loved dinosaurs, just like Grandpa. His grandpa was the best palaeontologist ever. He had been on telly and everything. Everyone knew him. Jack was going to be exactly like Grandpa when he grew up. He didn't care what his parents said. His father was a lawyer and always moaning about lawsuits and silly stuff like that. He was always working weekends and he never got home from work before eight o' clock at night. One of his clients had given him a black eye because he'd had to pay a huge fine. His dad said the likes of him should be locked up and the key thrown away forever. That didn't sound very nice. No, he definitely didn't want to be a lawyer.

His mum worked at the local supermarket. She said she didn't have to, but it was boring being stuck in all day with a young child. She said she could have been a lawyer, too, if she hadn't had Jack.

"A lawyer is a proper job, Jack," she always said.

"But I want to be a palaeontologist," Jack shouted back at her.

It wasn't fair. His mum always spoiled things. He wondered why she hated dinosaurs so much, but deep down he knew why.

Grandpa knew, too. It was because of his dad.

Grandpa said his dad had wanted to be a palaeontologist and was even better than he was. Jack didn't believe him. Grandpa knew everything there was to know about dinosaurs. It didn't matter. Grandma hadn't let him anyway. She made him go to a different college and become a lawyer instead.

Grandma sounded just like his mum. Sometimes he wished he had known Grandma but, at times like that, he was glad he didn't. It was bad enough with his mum nagging. But the crash had taken away the chance of him ever knowing Grandma.

He just wished his mum loved him as much as Keiran's mum loved Keiran. Keiran was his best friend. Keiran's mum was always telling Kerian she loved him and kissing him on the head. Kerian hated it, but Jack would have even given up George if his mum did that.

He thought his dad loved him. He often gave him a quick hug or a pretend thump on the shoulder. His dad played games with him, too. His mum was always too busy.

Grandpa loved him. Grandpa always kissed him on the head. Jack could cope with anything when Grandpa was around. But where was he? Jack needed him now. But he was gone. And he wasn't ever coming back.

***

Sunlight stabbed his eyes. Jack pushed the covers back and blinked as he squinted at the clock. Six o' clock. He had been asleep for hours. He had been dreaming, though it hadn't been a nice dream. A horrible man had come and taken him away to a room full of lawyers. They all had silly wigs on their heads like they were in fancy dress, only they weren't very good at it. Jack was good at fancy dress. He had found a brilliant dinosaur outfit for Keiran's birthday party. His mum had made him go as Mickey Mouse instead.

Jack reached out for George. George hated early mornings, especially Sunday mornings. Jack's lip quivered. George wasn't there. Then he remembered. He got out of bed and listened at the door. Silence. Poor George. He had been out in the garden all night. And on his own, too. George had never been on his own before. He would have been so frightened.

A loud snore came from his parents' room as Jack

crept past. He smiled. His mum always insisted she didn't snore.

"Jack!" his dad's voice was like thunder.

Jack swung round. There was no one there. He peered through the crack in the door. He could see his mum, her golden hair splayed out like an octopus over the pillow. He squinted, trying to see his dad's spiky hair. The pillow was empty.

A waterfall built to a crescendo as the toilet flushed. The tank rattled, a wheezing beast coming to claim him.

"All right then, Jack? What are you doing out of bed?" his dad was right behind him.

"I've lost George."

"We'll find him later. You had best go back to bed. You know your mum likes her lie-in."

Jack nodded, trying to fight the tears. He dragged himself back to his room. He couldn't bear it; he had to get George. A smile tugged at the corner of his mouth. He knew what to do. His dad could sleep on a pile of dinosaur bones. All he had to do was wait.

It felt like hours, but Jack knew only five minutes had gone by before his dad's silly snores started. It always made him laugh. His mum sounded like a train and his dad was more like a measly mouse.

Jack dared to move. He made it to the door and out to the landing. Then he saw her.

His mum barred his way, a T-rex moving in for the kill. She opened her mouth, her teeth long and sharp.

He blinked. Her image disappeared. He quickly ran down the stairs, sure he could hear her thudding behind him. *No!* Jack missed the last step, twisting his ankle as it connected with the banister. He clawed his way along the carpet, seeing the kitchen door ahead and beyond it, the back door and freedom.

Jack turned the key in the back door and peered round the doorframe. Nothing moved. He ducked back inside, pausing to strain his ears for noises from upstairs. He could hear a monster. It was making noises like a drill. He smiled, realising it was his own heart hammering.

He took one step outside. Then two. He walked on across the grass feeling the dew squelch between his toes.

His eyes roamed the vast garden, pausing on the pond halfway down and the rockery to the left. George wasn't there. His feet took him forward and he stopped by the birdbath. Someone was watching him. He froze. The hairs on his arms were standing to attention. Huge eyes were bearing down on him, coming closer. He could almost feel the stench of stale breath on his neck. He had known there were dinosaurs in the garden. His mum and dad didn't believe him.

A hiss, followed by claws clamping down on his foot. He screamed. Mister Jinks from next door grinned at him, licking his lips. The ginger feline turned tail and scrambled over the fence. Jack cringed. He hoped Mister Jinks hadn't eaten George for breakfast.

Jack quickly moved on to the greenhouse, his ankle forgotten. He peeped inside, but the stringy tomato plants were the only things there. He hurried on to the apple tree.

"George!" Jack knew the iguana had been there.

He remembered seeing the poor creature succumb to his mother's size eights the night before. Tears threatened to fall. He hoped she hadn't put George in the bin. Everything he loved went in the bin.

"Jack," a whisper hung in the air.

Jack grinned, surging forward. George needed him. He ran to the bottom of the garden, his feet flying over leaves and moss. A flash of brown. He could almost see George now.

It was the music that caught him unawares. Gentle, tinkling music floated towards him. Jack stopped, but his feet kept going. He put his arms out, a scream in his throat. He was too late. On and on he tumbled, through the hedge, sharp bracken clawing at him, through long, luscious grass and stony ground. He hit his head and everything went black.

When he awoke, dull pain spread over his body. He gulped, sure he was going to be sick. Then he didn't hurt any more. He looked around, his eyes focusing on the shack in the distance. The soft music was coming from inside.

Something else caught his eye. There were holes of freshly dug earth everywhere. He blinked. They were still there. Something was poking out of one of them. It couldn't be. It was. He scrambled forward and his hands dug like a digger on a building site. He squealed with delight, extracting a huge bone. He raised it above his head, triumphant.

Shivers shot up his spine. It was a Tyrannosaurus Rex. He was sure it was. It looked like the one in his dinosaur book. He dug again. Another bone, part of a tail this time and then a tooth and piece of skull. A very big skull.

Perhaps he would be on the telly, too. People would come from miles away to see his discovery. But he didn't care about that. All he cared about was Grandpa. Jack couldn't wait to tell Grandpa. He would be so proud.

"I always knew you could do it," Grandpa said.

For a moment, Jack thought Grandpa was really there. But Grandpa was dead. Perhaps he could tell his mum and dad. He could almost hear their voices.

"Don't be so stupid," his mum would say, "you're going to be a lawyer when you grow up. Now stop this nonsense."

Jack pushed his mum's image from his mind and turned to the next mound, his hands covered in dirt. He uncovered more bones, a different species this time.

"That's a Clarionosaurus, Jack. Wonderful. You have discovered a new dinosaur."

Jack's heart surged. He thought he was going to burst. He grinned and looked up. It *was* Grandpa. His grandpa had come back. He ran into his arms, letting the older man swing him round and round.

"I've been watching you, boy. I knew you could do it," Grandpa put him down on the ground and took his hand. "Come on, let's go inside."

"But what about the Clarionosaurus? And there are more dinosaurs, too."

"We've got plenty of time for that, Jack."

"Do you live here?" Jack asked, his eyes taking in the wooden shutters and pots full of plants.

He stared at the candyfloss clouds floating by and the setting sun, creating a peaceful, pink sky. Hundreds of birds were singing, joining in the sweet music. Butterflies as big as beach balls beat their wings in time to the rhythm.

"Yes, it's beautiful, isn't it?" Grandpa said, giving his hand a squeeze. "You'll love it here."

The soothing music grew louder, beckoning Jack forward. The young boy shivered, stepping through the door. His eyes lit up at the spread on the table. There were T-rex crisps and Diplodocus jelly and right in the middle was George. Jack grinned at his grandpa. He couldn't ever remember being so happy.

***

Mary was screaming. Cliff held her, his eyes spilling over with tears. He reached out and gently stroked the head of blond hair. His hand touched the gash, still fresh on the small forehead. In the distance, he was sure he could hear the sound of music.

FAIRIES

She's seeing things again. My dear, sweet Eleanor. I watch her, yearning to reach out my hand and stroke her long, brown hair, to tuck it back behind her ears. The tiny girl turns. She knows I am watching. Such sadness in those glorious eyes. My fingers are edging nearer. I stop. I can't touch her. I mustn't. My dear, sweet Eleanor, only seven years old.

She turns back and sobs, clutching her teddy. Dear teddy, so old and worn from constant hugs and tears trapped beneath the fading fur.

Her sobbing slows. She stops. Her head leans on one side and her fringe falls forward, hiding her face. She flings back her head and the smile twitches at the corner of her mouth. She listens and light illuminates her. Her eyes dance, alive once more and her thin fingers tap teddy to a tune only she can hear. They're here. Oh, Eleanor, the fairies have come again.

Her smile slowly spreads as mine vanishes. Her tears have dried and mine replace them. Why, Eleanor? Oh, why?

Her hands reach out and open up as if to catch a ball. She pulls back. She has one in her grasp. Yellow, pink, purple; only she knows the colour of the wings, the hue of the dress, the feel of hair and feet flitting over flesh. She turns to me and holds out her hand. I can't see them. I can't see them, Eleanor.

I turn away. I can bear no more. But I have to look back. Eleanor is dancing now, with her arms raised above her head and her eyes glancing gleefully in all directions. They're everywhere, aren't they? Eleanor won't look at me now. She doesn't need me any more, not when they're here. This is the only time she smiles, the only time she feels anything. Why, Eleanor? What terrible thing made you create such a wondrous world? Is the real word so terrible, so bad?

I am shaking with sobs now. I know the answer. I know the things Eleanor has seen.

Things a seven-year-old shouldn't see, shouldn't ever know anything about. And I could do nothing about it. I couldn't stop it; I couldn't save her.

But it wasn't always like this. Her daddy used to make her smile. All the time. He worked hard at the shop and came home as early as he could to read her a bedtime story. He used to bring sweets home every Friday. Fizzy cola bottles were the best. So sugary and sweet. Her daddy used to swing her round and round. Her mummy used to scold him for getting Eleanor all excited before bedtime and then he would pull out a bottle of perfume and Mummy would fling her arms around him in forgiveness. Her mummy didn't mind really. All she wanted was for her Eleanor to be happy. And they were happy. All of them. Such a happy family.

Then everything changed. It was all her daddy's fault. Horrible, horrible Daddy. Poor Eleanor. Poor Eleanor, who had been feeling sick all day at school and who had come home early with Mummy. Her mummy had gone to school straight from work when they couldn't get hold of Daddy at the shop. Her daddy had taken the afternoon off work and gone home to bed.

Dear Eleanor. She ran up the stairs when she saw

his car outside, all thoughts of sickness suddenly gone. Her fast footsteps didn't give Mrs Draper from number three much time to wrap Daddy's dressing gown round herself.

Her daddy shouted at Eleanor. He shouted at her like he had never shouted before. Her mummy came up after her. She was so shocked and so hurt. For a moment, her face had crumpled and the floor had threatened to claim her. Then anger kicked in. Anger at how Daddy had spoken to their daughter. Anger at Daddy for what he had done. Anger at Mrs Draper.

Her mummy told Eleanor to go downstairs while she marched on, pulling at Daddy's dressing gown. Eleanor didn't know what was going on. She thought her daddy was ill. Why else would he be in bed? Perhaps Mrs Draper was ill, too. But she knew something was wrong. It was in their voices and their faces.

Eleanor couldn't move. She watched the ugly folds of flesh emerge as the emerald green gown fell to the floor. She stood rigid as Daddy leapt up, pulling his trousers past his hips, and launched himself at her mummy. Mummy was wild, lashing out viciously and verbally.

Eleanor should have gone. She would have known what was to come next, but she wouldn't have seen it. It wouldn't have blasted into her conscious, day in, day out, until the only thing that made sense were the fairies.

The knife came from nowhere. Eleanor hadn't seen it before. All she saw was a shimmer of silver and then there was a sea of scarlet. Her mummy didn't even get a chance to scream. Mrs Draper did.

She screamed before she ran down the stairs and out of the house. She didn't even stop to pick up her clothes.

Eleanor is still now. She is holding out her arms, beckoning the fairies to her. But not scarlet ones. There won't be any scarlet fairies. Eleanor doesn't like scarlet.

I wish I could see them. I wish I could be there with Eleanor and feel the flutter of their wings. I wish they would invite me into their magical world and spare me my suffering. Eleanor is fading now. I can't see her. Come back, Eleanor, come back.

I look around the room. It is so bright, so stark, so empty. The people will be here soon. They think they are helping. I don't want their help. I don't want to remember the bad time. I want the fairies to come again. I used to see them. All colours of the rainbow and more besides. Except scarlet. I don't like scarlet. But they were my friends. For years and years. My only friends, apart from teddy.

The door opens. They're here.

"Come on, Eleanor, time for your medication."

I reach for my teddy. Perhaps one day the fairies will come back.

THE ESCAPE

I am falling, like the darkness. All around me are unfamiliar smells and sounds: unknown predators weaving their way towards me. I steady myself and make for the safe sanctuary of the tree as the rain begins to stab at my eyes. I gulp, listening to the wind, no longer the gentle breeze of the day.

"Sam. Sam." I'm sure I heard my name.

I know there's no one there. My captors will have missed me by now, but they won't find me. I am free at last.

"Sam. Sam." There it is again. I laugh. It's just the wind whistling through the tall grass.

I lie down on my makeshift bed of leaves and stare up at the vast branches above. I'm certain it's an oak; I think I can see the acorns dangling down. My hands touch the mulch and mud oozes its way under my nails. I flinch and sit up. It's only a worm gliding over my hands. I hope there aren't any rats. There's a squeak to my right. I scream. Small, scurrying feet fade.

My stomach churns, a mixture of fear and hunger. Crisps, chocolate, cheese, bread – images of fresh food flash through my mind. But I had no choice. I had to flee, there and then.

The dazzling moon shines its pale blue brightness through the branches. Shadows dance around me, tall figures looming closer. I lean against the tree and my fingers claw at the gnarled bark. I wish I could merge with its trunk.

I stifle a yawn and my heavy eyelids droop. Then jerk open. I can't sleep. They won't give up until they have me under lock and key once more. Eventually, my body takes over and I sink down onto my damp bed, the leaves squelching beneath.

A new brightness suddenly pricks my eyes. I battle to open them while the sun beams down on me to reveal a fresh new day. My aching body reminds me of my dreadful night's sleep. There is a staleness in my mouth and my tongue feels furry.

I struggle to my feet, my soggy clothes sticking to my body, their stench telling me they are more than two days old. Gagging, I stare down at them, an instant reminder that they aren't my clothes but a uniform. I hope no one can see me. I stand out like a fox amongst a pack of hounds.

I scan the horizon. My eyes come to rest on a farmhouse. I grin; I will have breakfast today. I run towards it, sure I can smell the sizzling bacon. I stop. I will have to be careful. I can picture the farmer and his wife now – dashing to the telephone as I lunge outside, away and to freedom once more.

I peer through the grimy window. The furniture, with its layer upon layer of dust, and the cobwebs swinging back and forth are an indication of the building's emptiness. I go to the back door and push; the ancient wood almost gives way at my touch. My fingers move quickly over the work surfaces. They fumble with the cupboard doors. My eyes are alive as a can of beans spills out onto the counter.

"Sam. Sam." The door creaks my name and gapes open.

I can't stay. The search will have started at dawn.

I can almost feel their presence. I grab the can, my eyes fast and furiously seeking a can opener. A noise upstairs. I freeze. Footsteps on the stairs. A tramp? Or is it them? Have they been lying in wait all along? The can crashes to the floor. I sprint to the door, fighting the thick cobwebs as a spider tries out its new home in my matted hair. Almost falling over my feet, I grab the doorframe, using the splintered wood to hold myself back.

"Looks like he came this way, Ted," a man's voice is close by, "let's check out that farmhouse."

I run back inside and crouch in a corner. Another sound on the stairs. The kitchen door bursts open. My knuckles turn white as my grip on the cupboard tightens. My eyes are wide, staring at the creature now in the same room.

The huge dog flies at me, its claws sharp and teeth clenched. I flinch, my arms covering my face. Nothing. I dare to look. As suddenly as it came, the wild beast has vanished through the back door. I collapse against the cupboard, catching a moment's breath, readying myself for the next fight.

The door bangs open. "Sam. Come on, Sam. We know you're in here. Don't make this any harder than it already is," the stern voice fails at pleasantries.

"We're a man down, Sam. That dog went for Ted in a big way. We just want to make sure you're okay," another, kinder this time.

I shan't be fooled. They don't care for me. A third set of footsteps enters the room.

"Sam, it's me. Look, son, enough is enough," a familiar voice now.

A tear pricks the corner of my eye. I blink it away.

I can't cry. I can't let them see me like this.

Images flick through my head – a warm bed, hot food, friendly faces, love. I stand up. Suddenly, I run forward, allowing myself to be hugged close, safe in the strong arms.

"Sam, we've been so worried about you. I wish you had said you weren't happy at boarding school instead of running away. Come on, son. Let's get you home to Mum," Dad says.

I grin at him, my days as a fugitive firmly over.

A SPECIAL HELPER

How I wished Mum wasn't so grumpy. She always used to smile – a great, big grin of a smile. Instead, she just looked sad all the time. And cross.

I asked her if she would play snakes and ladders with me. It was my favourite game. She shouted at me. Her mouth gaped open as wide as wide can be, just like the snakes in my game. I thought her tongue was going to come creeping out and that she was going to swallow me – whole. But she didn't. Her mouth clamped shut and then she cried. She kept saying she was sorry over and over again.

I just wanted her to be like she used to be. She always played with me then. Not that she was very good. She didn't ever win. She was quite useless really.

"Oh no, back down that snake I go. You're too good for me, Oliver," she would laugh.

And I'd look into her eyes and they were so bright. Not any more. I didn't think anyone's eyes could be so dull. I hoped they became bright again.

Like they were when she watched me play football. She hadn't been for ages. She said she wasn't up to it. Dad still went. But it wasn't the same. I wasn't great at football. I wanted to be, but I always seemed to miss the goal.

"Come on, Oliver, you can do better than that," Dad always shouted, just like he did at the England players on the TV during the World Cup.

Mum didn't mind. She said if I was having fun it

didn't matter. She just looked proud of me, whatever.

I thought she would be proud of me when I did well in my test at school. I couldn't wait to tell her.

"I've done it. I got the highest marks, Mum!" I said.

I'd never done that before. I looked up at her and waited to see the excitement in her face. It wasn't there. She didn't care.

"Good. That's good," she said.

But I knew she didn't mean it. I could see it there in her face. No, she didn't mean it at all. She didn't mean anything any more.

"I didn't mean to shout at you," she said, a lot.

It was like she was a different person sometimes. And then she would almost remember who she was. I thought an alien might have come down in the night, taken my mum away and put a clone in her place. I'd read about it in my space comic and my friend, Tom, at school, said it happened sometimes. It was a daft idea really. She was definitely my mum. Just a grumpier mum than she used to be.

Tom said it could have been because of the dreaded 'D' word. Half of the parents in my class at school had gone through the 'D' word. I knew my mum and dad weren't. They argued, but that was nothing new. Dad still walked through the house in his dirty work boots, left stuff lying on the floor in every room and got silly after a beer or two. And Mum still nagged him, exactly like she had always done.

One thing changed, though. They cuddled each other a lot more. Well, it was Dad cuddling Mum really. When grown-ups cuddled, it definitely meant they weren't going to do the 'D' word.

I thought about asking Mum what was wrong. And then Gran got ill. She had cancer and was really poorly. Gran was grumpy, too, and sick. I wondered if Mum had cancer. Perhaps she was going to start being sick, too. I couldn't ask Mum. I wasn't sure if I really wanted to know whether she was ill. Then Gran died. I didn't want Mum to die.

But I started thinking, what would I do if she did die and I hadn't talked to her about it? What would I do if one day she was just gone? We used to talk about everything.

"There's nothing you can't tell me," she used to say.

And she was right. Well, almost. I mean, you can't tell your mum everything, can you? I told her when there was a boy at school who was sometimes nasty and sometimes nice. I played with him when he was nice and it was great fun. Suddenly, he'd change and be all horrible. Sometimes he tried to make me be horrible, too.

"When he's like that, just walk away," Mum said. "Tell him you don't want to be his friend if he's going to be like that."

I did exactly what she said and it worked. I think it did him good, too. He wasn't nearly so horrible after that.

I liked telling Mum nearly everything. We talked about the moon and the planets far, far away. About being a fireman when I grew up and about not liking girls, except her of course. So I had to tell her about this, but I didn't always say things very well.

"Are you going to die?" I asked her one morning

at breakfast.

I put my hand straight over my mouth. I kept it there for ages, wishing I hadn't said those words as I stared at Mum. She looked like she was going to be sick and her eyes looked like they were going to leap out of her head. And then she did something I didn't expect. She smiled.

"No, Oliver, I'm not going to die. Don't worry, I'm not sick like Gran. But…" She stopped smiling.

"Are you an alien? Have your people got my real mum?" Even I couldn't believe I had said it.

But I was glad I did. Because she laughed. A lot. She tipped her head back and her shoulders shook. I thought she was still laughing. She wasn't. She was crying.

"I'm sorry," she said, sniffing. "I'm not an alien, though I feel a bit like one at the moment. And like I said, I'm not sick like Gran and I'm not going to die, but I am ill, Oliver."

If she wasn't ill like Gran, what was wrong with her? There weren't such things as grumpyitus or crying disease. And that's what seemed to be wrong with her.

I opened my mouth to ask her some more, but Dad came into the room. He didn't look very happy at all. I wondered if maybe Mum's illness was catching. Though, Dad didn't keep crying like Mum and he didn't stay grumpy for long.

I thought about asking Dad about Mum's illness. I wasn't sure if he'd tell me. Mum treated me like a big boy most of the time, but I'm sure Dad thought I was still three years old.

As it turned out, I didn't have to ask him. When I

was reading to him one night, he took the book from me and put it down.

I looked up at him and he was chewing his lip. He started to say something. And stopped. Started again. Stopped.

"Tell me, Dad. Please," I said.

"We should have told you a long time ago, Oliver," he said, with a bit of a frown and a bit of a smile at the same time. "We didn't know how to. You must have been wondering what on earth was going on, but it came so suddenly and we didn't know how to deal with it."

"Do you mean Daisy?" I asked.

Dad laughed. "No, no, Oliver. Daisy didn't come suddenly at all. We were all prepared for Daisy. Though, sometimes, she's quite hard to deal with."

I nodded. I had wanted a brother for ages and ages. A sister came along instead. I tried not to think about her too much, especially when she was sick and when she filled her nappy. Her latest thing was grabbing my cheek. But she could be quite cute at times. Not that I told anyone that.

"So Mum's not grumpy because of Daisy?"

"In a roundabout way, I suppose she is. Your mum's got an illness that sometimes happens after having a baby. It's called postnatal depression," Dad said.

"But I know the word depressed. I've tried to cheer Mum up and stop her feeling depressed, but it hasn't worked."

"Unfortunately, there's a bit more to this illness," Dad said.

"But I don't want her to have this... post whatever

depression. I want her to be happy," I said and then it was me crying.

I didn't hear the door. I didn't see Mum walk over, but I felt her hand on my shoulder. I tried to look at her. She was smiling. Not quite that great, big grin of a smile but almost.

"I will be happy, Oliver. I won't have this illness forever. The doctor says I'm getting better. But I need a special helper, that little bit of extra help. It won't be easy. I'll be grumpy, I'll cry, I'll shout and wail, but with that special help, it'll go away. Do you think you can be that helper, Oliver?" she asked.

I nodded and held her tight.

It took a bit of time for the illness to go. But we worked at it – together. Dad, too. I felt a bit lost at first when Mum didn't need her special helper any more, but then Daisy started crawling, so Mum really did need a special helper again.

THE RETURN

Sarah screamed. Pain tore through her. She clutched at her stomach. Panic. Fear. Wide-eyed and full of terror, she stared at the violent sea, watching the waves thrashing closer and closer.

She took a deep breath. The pain ebbed away, together with the waves. All was calm once more. She shivered; the memories refused to be banished. Clamping her eyes shut, she forced the images of the stricken child to disappear. Her eyes flew open. The girl had gone.

Sarah watched the waves gently tumble in to shore. Her toes tingled as the freezing waters lapped over them. She smiled, longing for an exotic beach and warm waters. The sun pounded down on her bare shoulders and sweat oozed from her brow, but the sea remained cold. It was England after all. She patted her bulging stomach, her thoughts returning to the cool waters.

Twenty years ago. Was it really that long? She hadn't thought she would ever return and yet, here she was. She thought she had forgotten, but she would never forget.

The girl's hair was dark and tied in bunches. Her huge brown eyes were wide behind long lashes and rosebud lips quivered as tears splashed onto her pink polka dot swimsuit. Sarah remembered it clearly. It had been her fifth birthday.

The day had started so well. It was to be a fresh start. A new beginning, her parents had said. They'd lied.

Sarah could remember her excitement, her joy as she had sat in the car, slowly edging nearer and nearer to the delightful salty smell of the sea. The usual bank holiday traffic was of no concern to a little girl and she had almost managed to block out the shouting. Almost.

She recalled her disappointment when they had finally arrived. The weathermen were wrong. The beautiful day they had promised had vanished. The early morning sun had been shrouded behind bulging rain clouds. Sarah stood, a silent, lone figure on the beach, savouring the feel of the water between her toes. The sea had seemed to call her, beckoning her to enter it, singing to her that it would keep her safe. Her legs carried her onwards, further and further.

Her parents' screeches gradually faded. Would they notice if she slipped away? Her mother and father didn't care about her anyway. They wouldn't be getting a divorce if they cared. Mother had promised they weren't, said they were going to give things another try. But she knew all about divorce. The children at school talked about it all the time.

Suddenly, she hadn't felt so safe. Fierce rain stung her eyes and the waves gathered their force. The wind whistled and the chilly waters threatened to devour her. The taste had sickened her as the waters gushed into her mouth. The smell of seaweed was vile as it wrapped itself around her, tight, and the sea tried to claim her as its prize.

Hands grabbed her, dragging her to safety. She spluttered, choking and screaming for air. It was too late, she was certain. She had blinked, wondering if she was in heaven.

Her breathing eased. It was okay. She was safe. She'd survived. Sarah remembered their arms around her that day. Arms she hadn't felt for a long time. She had smiled, relishing the feel of their love for her. Mother, father and child. A family once more.

It hadn't lasted. The divorce was inevitable.

***

"Mummy! Mummy!"

The cries brought Sarah back to the present. She smiled, almost knocked from her feet as her son and daughter launched themselves into her arms. Her breath caught in her throat. She stared at the man walking towards her. He joined them, his strong arms encircling the threesome.

Sarah closed her eyes, feeling his love envelop her. She smiled at her husband and down at her children, her hands coming to rest on her stomach, thankful that heaven had decided to wait.

THE HACKER

The front door slammed shut.

"That you, Ron?" came a screech over the TV chant of 'Jerry, Jerry'.

Ron kicked his *Dr Martens* off and thumped up the stairs two at a time, choosing, as usual, to ignore his mum. He shoved his shoulder into his bedroom door and a grin almost touched his thin lips as it thwacked against the wall. One shove with his elbow and it was firmly closed once more. He breathed in the stale scent of cigarette smoke, sweat, mouldy food and *Avon* aftershave. He smiled; he loved his room.

He lay back on his bed and stared up at the custard-coloured ceiling and the smile slowly left his face. What a waste of a morning. He hated the idiots at the Job Centre, all sat there behind their computers with their smiley faces and stupid ideas. The smarmy bloke in the suit and *Homer Simpson* tie had been no different today.

"So, have I got this right? You left school three years ago, aged eighteen, with no qualifications and you've had twenty-three jobs in the last two years, the longest lasting three days?"

"If that's what I've written on the form, then that's what it is or are you calling me a liar?" Ron had said and pushed his chair back, his mouth contorting into his best sneer and his fists clenching.

"No, sir, of course I'm not calling you a liar. I'm sure I can find the ideal job for you."

Ideal job, indeed. Bog cleaner or, as the suit so eloquently put it, 'lavatory attendant'.

"Have you thought about becoming a refuse collector, sir? The pay isn't bad in the trade."

Trade? Collecting other people's muck and filth was a trade? Pah! There was no way he was going anywhere near other people's wheelie bins.

Ron sighed, his thoughts coming back to the present. He knew just what he wanted to do. Computers. Or, as the suit called it, 'IT'. And he was good at computers, too. But they wouldn't let him do it. They said he wasn't qualified, that companies couldn't take that sort of a risk.

He swung his legs off the end of the bed and pushed himself to his feet. He walked over to the desk and chair, his eyes falling greedily on the computer. He'd show them.

Ron pressed the button and the computer hummed into life. He rubbed his hands together. What would it be today? The Job Centre? A bank? Scotland Yard? No, he had done all those before. What about the FBI? Yes, it was about time he faced a challenge.

He laughed as he logged on, his fingers flicking over the keys. He typed in his password, 'IRRHNO1*' – 'I' for Invincible, then 'R' for Ron, another 'R' for Rules, an 'H' for Hacker, 'N' for Number, 'O' for One, followed by the '1' and '*', just to make sure of his status.

He sat back, waiting for the golden gates of the internet to open themselves to him. He licked his lips in anticipation of what he might find.

Ron had already learned so much, seen things that would shock other people. Bank balances of the rich and famous, government plans for the next five years and, if the King knew all the things he had discovered about him, he would have no hair left, never mind it going grey.

He didn't know what he was going to do with it all yet, though making money figured prominently on his list. He'd have to go to the papers. They would love it and pay him a fortune. He grinned at the thought of them fighting over his story. Oh, and how many stories he had. Lots of them. Even about some of the newspaper goons themselves.

Then he wouldn't have to go to the Job Centre any more. He could tell them all where to stick their precious jobs. He could just sit back and let the money roll in. Perhaps he would buy a new house. Or two houses. One for him and one for his mum, get her out of the council house she had been stuck in all her life. She could be a pain in the backside at times, especially since his dad had left ten years ago, but she wasn't a bad old girl really.

He would buy himself one of the latest computers on the market, too – one that did everything. His was all right. It did the job, but it was old now, took too long to do everything.

Ron's fingers moved skilfully once more. The FBI. He had seen the movies. They were like the suits at the Job Centre, who thought they were above everyone else, but the FBI had flashy badges and gleaming guns. They weren't ready for Ron Whiting, though.

'You are entering an unauthorized website.' Ron waited for the words to explode onto the screen. He loved it. 'Authorized users only. Type in username and password.'

He grinned. This was the best bit. And so easy, he may as well already be in.

"Burp! Oh dear. Excuse me," the voice was little more than a whisper. "Too much fizzy water at lunch."

"Who's that?" Ron swung round.

There was no one there. He must be imagining things. He turned back to the task at hand.

"Ronald Whiting, I have been sent to deal with you by the Great Fairy Computer King. He is most upset at your dishonest undertakings," the voice again.

"Undertakings? Are you having a laugh, Mum? You know you're not allowed in here."

Ron's eyes searched the room. His mum wasn't exactly the skinniest of women and there weren't that many places to hide. Ron rubbed his eyes. Too many late nights on the object in front of him. Perhaps he would have an early night.

He looked at the screen. Something was flitting about in the top left-hand corner. He squinted. It had wings and a silly tiara. And a pink tutu thing. What was that? It looked like a wand. He squinted again. It *was* a wand – and she was a fairy. What on earth was a fairy doing on the FBI website? He swore. A virus.

"By the authority invested in me by the Great Fairy Computer King, if you do not desist in your unlawful activities immediately, I shall have no choice…"

"Sod off," Ron shouted.

"That's it," the fairy said and pointed her wand at him. Stars shimmered, slowly snaking towards him.

He blinked. Who was he? What was his name? And what was he doing? He looked at the screen. FBI. What did the letters FBI stand for? Furry Badger Incorporation? Ron shook his head. He didn't feel like looking at the computer any more. But how did he switch it off? With that thing that looked like a keyboard, with letters and numbers all over? Ron pressed the keys, any keys, and they beeped back at him. It was a bit of a useless keyboard. Perhaps he would go and make a cup of tea for his mum. Yes, he remembered her. A wonderful woman who he loved very much.

He walked down the stairs and found her in the lounge.

"Fancy a cuppa, Mum?" he asked, smiling.

His mum's jaw dropped.

"How about a choccy biccy to go with it? You deserve a treat."

She just nodded her head.

An hour later and Ron's usual charm had returned. "What on earth am I doing sat here with you?" he asked, staring at his mum. "Get your arm off me, woman. And what are we watching? *Frozen*? I must be going mad."

He pushed himself off the sofa and stomped upstairs. He walked over to the computer and sat down, clicking the mouse and ending the computer's temporary doze. Ron knew he had been doing something extremely important. He had been about to crack a code. But whose code?

The nursery rhyme *Three Blind Mice* popped into his head. He tried to force it out. Three blind… No, it was four… FB… FBI! That was it.

Something in the top left-hand corner caught his eye. Something he had seen somewhere before.

"I see the order from the Great Fairy Computer King has had no impact upon you at all," the fairy said, hands on hips, "I shall have no alternative but to place a permanent punishment order upon you."

"Well, fairy, I shall have no alternative but to wipe you out for good. Blimey, you would think the FBI could come up with something better than this," Ron said, raising his eyes to the ceiling as he set about ridding his screen of the intrusive fairy.

Half an hour later and she was still there.

"Nothing's beaten me before. Get lost, fairy!" Ron tapped away.

"You simply don't understand, do you? I have nothing to do with this FBI. I have been sent here by the order of the Great Fairy Computer King."

"I'm not listening."

"I'm sorry to hear that, Ronald. Just when I was beginning to enjoy myself, though the Great Fairy Computer King has many like you for me to deal with. Goodbye, Ronald." The fairy smiled and waved her wand.

A bolt of lightning flashed from the wand and flew straight at Ron. Thunder bounced round the room before blasting Ron's ears. Stars, moons and fluffy white clouds appeared before his eyes. Then darkness and nothing.

Ron opened his eyes and yawned. He smiled; he'd been having such a lovely dream. He couldn't remember it exactly, but he felt such a huge sense of wellbeing and joy.

Ron looked round his room. What a mess. He had

better tidy it all up. He picked up files and folders littered across the floor. He looked at the covers – banks and building societies, the local police and Job Centre. Those definitely needed to go in the shredder. And thinking about the Job Centre, he'd have to get an early night. Was it 9.00 or 9.30 they opened? Whichever, he would be there on the dot. And while he was at it, perhaps he would enrol on a college course.

 He looked at his watch. Just enough time to start the dinner. A nice roast, for the best mum in the world, with sweet potatoes and baby peas. Perfect.

STRANGER

"Mummy! Daddy! Come in. You've got to come in. It's lovely and warm," Sally said, splashing in the sea.

"In a minute, dear." Mummy turned the page of her book.

"Daddy, hurry up," Sally said. "Daddy!"

"He's gone to sleep." Mummy prodded him in the ribs.

"What? Mmm," Daddy mumbled. Within seconds his body succumbed to sleep once more.

Sally turned her back on them. They never wanted to play. It wasn't fair. Her eyes roamed the miles of beach, taking in the brothers and sisters making magnificent sandcastles and chasing each other in and out of the sea. She wished she wasn't an only child. She didn't want a brother, though. No, she wanted a sister. But she would never have a sister. Her mother always said one was enough.

Something thwacked her on the back of the head. "Ow!" A beach ball bounced away. She swung round, ready to face her assailant. Instead, she smiled, watching as a little boy sidled up to her.

"Mummy says I have to say sorry," he said, blushing.

"Would you like to play catch?" Sally grinned at him.

"No, thank you. Mummy says I mustn't play with strangers," he said, grabbing his ball back and moving further down the beach.

Sally stared after him, her eyes filling with tears. "I'm not a stranger. Children aren't strangers. I'm only six. Oh, I hate you. I didn't want to play with you anyway," she shouted after him.

She folded her arms and stomped towards her parents.

"Mummy?"

"What now, Sally?"

"Nothing," Sally said, blinking back the tears and running into the sea. She relished the feel of the warm waters as they lapped over her.

"Help! Help!"

Sally's eyes widened. Where was it coming from? There – a boy and a girl were fighting over a spade. But no, the cry of help wasn't coming from them. Her eyes turned in the other direction. A man was running into the sea, with his arms wrapped around a young woman as he carried her laughing and giggling towards the gentle waves. Not them either.

"Help! Help!"

Finally, Sally saw her. Straight ahead. She looked so small, so far away, with her arms thrashing wildly and her head bobbing in and out of the water. Everyone remained oblivious to the girl's distress.

"Help. Please," Sally said, "she's drowning."

No one heard her. Sally ploughed forward, her doggy paddle fast and furious. Her swimming teacher wouldn't be very pleased with her. They had spent hours doing front crawl, but Sally hated front crawl. Doggy paddle was much better.

"I knew you would save me." The girl reached out and grabbed Sally's neck.

Sally slowly eased her back to shore. She was sure

the girl had been farther out to sea. They collapsed onto the sand, both gasping for breath.

"Are you okay?" Sally asked, looking the girl up and down. She couldn't stop staring. The girl looked so silly.

"Yes, I'm fine, thank you," the girl said, grinning.

Sally couldn't take her eyes from the girl's swimming cap. It looked like a huge daisy. They had to wear swimming caps at school, but there was no way she'd wear one on holiday. And not one as silly as that. Her eyes moved down to the girl's swimming costume. It was like something Great-Granny Edith wore.

"You know who I am, don't you?" the girl asked, excited.

"No."

"I knew I was right to come. They said it wasn't time yet, but I had to see you. And you need me. See, you're staring at me again. You do know me. Oh, Violet, it's so good to see you."

"I'm not Violet. My name's Sally. You must have me mixed up with someone else. Where are your mummy and daddy? They'll be looking for you."

"They're not here."

"They must be. You can't be here on your own."

"I'm not on my own. Anyway, I'm Gertrude."

"That's a funny name."

"No, it's not. Come on," Gertrude took her hand. "Do you want to play?"

"Oh, yes please." Funny fluttering feelings of excitement surged in her tummy. "Let's pretend we're mermaids."

"I love mermaids. They're so beautiful," Gertrude

said as they ran off, giggling.

***

Tom jolted awake. Something was wrong. He looked up at Joy, still engrossed in her steamy novel.
"Where's Sally?" he asked, his blue eyes scanning the scene.
"What? Hang on, I've just reached a good bit."
"I can't see her, Joy."
"I'm sure she's all right. Look what you've made me do. I've lost my page now. Don't fuss, Tom. You know she likes to be on her own... Oh, my goodness. She's up there on those rocks. Do something, Tom."
They were on their feet immediately, sprinting in the direction of the crags. They weaved round the path, higher and higher, eventually reaching the top.
"Sally? She's not here." Tom frowned.
"She has to be. What if she's fallen?" Joy yelled, "Sally, where are you?"
"Look, Gertrude," Sally came into view, "I think Mummy and Daddy have come to play."
"Sally, get over here right now," Joy said sternly, grabbing her daughter's hand.
"You mustn't play near the rocks." Tom joined them.
"But Gertrude said it would be all right."
"Who on earth's Gertrude?" Tom asked.
"Gertrude's my friend. She's right here," Sally said, pointing.
"There's no one there. Come on, let's get back to the beach," Joy said, striding onwards.
Ten minutes later, Joy was reunited with her book

and Tom lay sprawled on the sun-lounger.

"You stay there, Sally, just where we can see you," Tom said.

Sally pouted and looked the other way.

"You don't think she's invented one of those imaginary friends, do you?" Tom looked at his wife.

She thrust her book aside. "I hope not. Do you think she's happy? We work all day and then when we are together as a family, we do our own thing. We can't do this to her. Things have got to change."

"I don't think she's been happy for a while," Tom said, hanging his head. "Her teacher said she was a bit of a loner. She suggested we have another child. What a cheek, eh? We haven't time for more kids. As it is, the boss said I'll have to do more overtime soon."

"There's more to life than money and work, Tom."

***

"I didn't mean to get you into trouble," Gertrude said.

"That's okay. They're always like that. Can we play again?"

"I can't. I've got to go now, Violet."

"I'm Sally. How many times do I have to tell you? I don't know a Violet."

"Yes, you do. You wouldn't have been able to see me otherwise. And thank you for saving me. I knew you would do it this time. You tried so hard before, sister," Gertrude said, hugging Sally close.

Sally closed her eyes, and goosebumps danced a

merry jig over her body. She could see Gertrude in her mind, her screams growing louder and louder. But she wasn't in the sea. She was in the river, swirling round and round, as a whirlpool whipped itself into a frenzy, trying to suck her into its depths. The dark brown eyes pleaded, begging to be saved. Sally gasped as her own image joined Gertrude. Her arms reached for the girl, her cries filling the air.

But she couldn't have been there. She hadn't met Gertrude before that day. And yet, it was her. Her own face, her own eyes, her nose and lips. She was wearing a silly dress and her hair was tied back like Dorothy in *The Wizard of Oz*. Gertrude was shouting to her, calling her Violet. Gertrude's image faded and Sally was standing in a churchyard, rain beating down on her as a coffin was lowered into the ground. She was distraught, her world crashing down.

Then she was at school, the desk beside her empty. The picture blurred and she was sitting in a row, her fingers tapping at what appeared to be an ancient keyboard. But there was no computer screen. Another image, this time in a beautiful white dress, surrounded by people. And there was a man, so handsome, standing beside her.

Children came next. One, two, three, followed by four. On and on the images came until darkness and no more. But there was someone missing. There had always been someone missing.

"I tried. I wanted to save you so much. The current was too strong." Sally shivered, opening her eyes. "But I don't understand. I'm Sally and I don't have a sister."

Gertrude smiled, a familiar smile Sally saw each

time she looked in the mirror. "Shh. There, there. Everything will be all right."

"You're not coming back, are you?" Sally started to cry.

"When the time's right, I shall be back. Not like this, though. You won't recognise me, but you'll know me. I will be back. Goodbye, sweet sister. Goodbye."

Sally stood alone. All around her, people packed their things away as the sun slowly set and stomachs grumbled. The wind whipped round her ankles and she turned towards her parents, smiling as they caught sight of her.

"Mummy, Daddy." She ran over to them, her arms open wide. "When am I going to have a sister?"

"A what?"

"A sister. I'm going to have a sister."

Grins broke out on each parent's face.

"Not just yet, Sally. Not just yet."

Sally prodded her mother's stomach. She was sure it hadn't been that big earlier.

THE HOLIDAY

Emma listened to her teacher and cringed. She knew just what Miss Mills was going to say.

"I want you all to keep a diary of your holiday and hand it in to your new teacher, Mr Meagan, in six weeks' time. He wants to learn all about you," she said, beaming round the classroom.

"I'm going to Disneyland," someone yelled.

"I'm going to Majorca," another voice.

"That's wonderful. You'll have so much to write about," Miss Mills said.

The bell rang and that was it. Year three over. Emma walked through the school gates and tried to ignore her mum who was waving her arms wildly like an out of control windmill.

"How about that then? The end of term, Emma. Six lovely long weeks ahead of you. You shan't know what to do with yourself," her mum chuckled and ruffled Emma's hair.

Emma scowled and folded her arms. She marched on ahead, blinking away a flurry of tears. It wasn't fair. Her mum was right; she didn't know what to do with herself. Her best friend was flying off to Barbados. It looked fantastic in the brochure. Tim next door was going to the Isle of Man, which Emma didn't really like the sound of, but Tim was very excited about it all the same, and her cousin was going camping in France, which had to be lots and lots of fun. And what were they doing? Nothing. Going nowhere. Not even to the zoo for the day or to see the latest film at the cinema. It just wasn't fair.

A hand touched her shoulder. Emma turned round to face her mum, who was chewing her lip.

"Perhaps I can get a day off. Take you to the park. Or maybe your dad will have one of his good days. If he takes his stick, he might be all right. He won't be able to push the roundabout or chase you round like he used to, but... but..."

Emma took her hand and they walked in silence. It wasn't her mum and dad's fault. Not really. If anything was to blame, it was the stairs.

Dad had been in a rush, as usual. He hated getting up in the mornings and that Monday had been no exception. His workmate, Dan, had already hooted his horn three times. So Dad had kissed her on the cheek and said goodbye before leaping down the stairs two at a time.

He always said he couldn't remember much about what happened next. Just that he found himself at the bottom of the stairs in a crumpled heap, agonising pain shooting up his spine. The doctors didn't know what was wrong with his back. They sent him to specialists and something called the pain clinic. Nothing worked. In the end, they said there was nothing they could do: he would have to learn to live with it.

He had, just about. He could be a bit grumpy at times and he couldn't work any more. Mum had to do that instead, but cleaning jobs didn't pay very much, even though she always seemed to be at work. She said it was hard trying to feed and clothe them and pay the bills. There wasn't anything left for luxuries like holidays.

It all seemed so much worse as no one believed her dad. Emma did. She saw him struggle to get out of bed in the mornings and heard his shouts echo round the walls of the loo when he got stuck. As she packed her lunchbox each morning, she watched him stretch, trying to will some movement into his back, his eyes watering with the sheer effort and pain.

No one cared. Even his old workmates said he didn't want to work. But he did. He always squeezed her mum's hand as she dashed to work first thing and again late afternoon. His eyes would follow her weary body through the door and then he would hang his head while her aching feet scrunched up the lane.

Her mum needed a holiday. Her dad needed a holiday. She needed a holiday. Nothing fancy. Just a few days by the sea or in the countryside.

"Perhaps we'll be able to go on holiday next year," Mum said, unlocking the front door. "Your dad's having some good days now."

Emma looked into her mum's face. She wondered who she was trying to convince the most. It didn't matter anyway. They both knew his bad days far outweighed his good.

Emma ran on into the lounge. The sound of applause greeted her from the TV set. She smiled, seeing her father dozing on the sofa. Cricket did that to her, too.

She joined her mum in the kitchen.

"I'll be off in ten minutes. Tell your dad not to wait up. Mr Lee's got some overtime for me tonight. I'm afraid it's beans on toast again. I'll go shopping tomorrow, love."

Emma nodded.

"Look, the sun's come out at last. Why don't you have a play outside? I'll mow the lawn tomorrow as well. It looks like a jungle out there, doesn't it? Watch out for the tigers."

Emma hugged her mum and kissed her goodbye. She then ran to the back door and into the garden. They didn't have a garden with swings and slides and swimming pools like lots of her friends, but she wasn't one for all that. She liked digging. Her mum said she almost dug down to Australia when she was small. Emma didn't think she had, but perhaps she could do a bit of weeding as well. Make it look nice when her mum woke up the next day.

Emma grabbed the spade and trowel from the shed and set to work.

"Hello," a voice behind her made her jump.

No one ever came into their garden. Slowly, she turned round. It was a girl of about the same age. She was dressed in bright blue shorts and a brilliant yellow T-shirt. She had a bucket and spade in her hands and she couldn't stop smiling.

"I'm going to build the most gigantic sandcastle you've ever seen. Would you like to come with me?" she asked. "I'm Rosie, by the way."

Emma had often wished she had a sister. And that sister would have been called Rosie. Emma's smile was almost as wide as Rosie's. She eagerly got to her feet and took Rosie's hand. In no time at all, they were at the seaside, splashing in the salty sea and letting the sand trickle through their fingers. They made an enormous sandcastle and finished off the day with a delicious fish and chip supper.

It was over far too soon and Emma found herself

back in the garden. She hurried indoors to cook the beans and grill the toast for her dad. As she carried the tray in to him, she still couldn't stop smiling. She hoped Rosie came to see her the next day.

Rosie did. And the next day and the one after that. They went to see a circus one day, marvelling at the acrobats flinging themselves high in the air and gasping at the knife thrower hurling knives at incredible speed. A day was spent in the city, seeing all the touristy sights and taking in the tremendous array of toys in all the shops.

Another time, they had the best seats in the cinema and scoffed tubs full of popcorn and sweets. The days passed so quickly. Some days, Rosie didn't come and Emma spent time with her dad. Her mum managed to take a few days off work and they all went to the park.

One day, her mum made Emma cry as she'd managed to save up some money so they could have a day out at the safari park. Dad couldn't come because he couldn't walk far or stand up for too long, but Emma and her mum had a terrific time.

Emma loved her days with Rosie, too. They ran on and on through meadows full of flowers and fed animals at the farm park. Her school diary was bursting.

She knew it all had to come to an end and all too soon, it did. When she walked through the gates on the first day of term, she felt a touch of sadness. Rosie had gone now and Emma didn't think she would ever come back.

"Hi, Emma," her best friend said, running up to her.

"How was Barbados?" Emma asked.

"Awful. They had a hurricane. We were locked in our hotel room for most of the two weeks. I don't think anyone had a good time this year. Someone said they had food poisoning in Disneyland and Tim said it rained every day on the Isle of Man."

Emma gripped her diary. It looked like she'd had the best holiday this year.

"Thanks, Rosie. Thanks, Mum. Thanks, Dad," she murmured under her breath.

Smiling broadly, she thumped her diary onto Mr Meagan's desk. She thought about her dad. He'd had his old spark back recently and over the last couple of weeks he hadn't had to use his stick as much. Perhaps they would be going on holiday next summer. Though, it would have to be pretty fantastic to beat the summer she'd just had.

RICHARD EDWARDS

I never knew what happened to Richard Edwards. It never struck me to care.

We had all been larking about in the playground. Soldiers, I think we were playing, or maybe we were Daleks – the usual thing six-year-old boys who grew up in the seventies loved.

There was a group of us – me, Danny, Neil, Sam and Richard. We didn't know why Richard hung around with us. None of us really liked him, but he didn't seem to have any other friends. Maybe we just felt sorry for him.

I can remember seeing his empty chair during registration the next day.

"Has anyone seen Richard?" Miss Watkins peered at us over her thick glasses. "What about you, Michael? I saw you playing with him yesterday."

It took me a moment to realise she had said my name.

"What? Oh, no. No, Miss. I only saw him at lunchtime. He said he was going out after school. I don't know where," I replied, returning to my daydream about cars.

The police came and asked us lots of questions. We were all scared. We didn't know what was going on. All we knew was that Richard didn't come back to school again.

"What do you think happened to him?" I asked.

"I dunno. Don't care. At least he's not hanging round us now. He always smelt anyway. Perhaps he didn't want to go to school any more. He was weird. And he was a cry baby," Sam stated.

"I think he's dead," I offered.

"Dead? Only really old people die. People who are over thirty." Sam scoffed at my ignorance.

"My mum and dad say he's dead. Something nasty happened to him. Like it will to you if you don't stop being stupid," I challenged Sam.

We didn't talk about it after that. A new boy came and sat in Richard's chair. We forgot all about him.

But everyone soon knew what had happened to Richard Edwards. Well, the adults anyway. It was front page news throughout the country. Everyone had thought he would come home safe and sound. No one thought the unthinkable could have happened.

The children were protected. We weren't allowed to know Richard's fate. Not a day could have gone by without his parents thinking of him, but I didn't. I didn't give him a moment's thought. Until now. Now I care.

Oh, how I care. I think about him all the time. I torture myself, thinking over and over what that poor boy must have gone through.

I looked back through old records, searching for the capture of the killer, but he'd escaped, able to maim again on another day.

I hated the police. They hadn't done enough. They should have caught him, stopped him from his killing spree that spanned two decades. If they had, I would still have my daughter, my beloved Lucy.

She's only five years old, not even been at school for five months. She hasn't had a chance at life. How can I bear it if it's all been taken away?

I can see her clearly: her long, blonde plaited hair, her bright blue eyes full of fun and laughter and her cheeky smile. Surely no one could hurt such a princess.

The search for her has lasted four days. There is no hope. I know she's dead. Maybe if I had listened to Richard, made an effort to be his friend, he and Lucy would be here now. You see, Richard was the killer's first victim.

I know it's not my fault, though. I couldn't stop such an evil person. He would have chosen another victim, another poor child.

"Oh, Alice. Why aren't you here?" I stare at my wife's photo. "I can't bear to lose you both."

My mobile rings. I snatch it up.

"I've got some news for you, Michael," Inspector Chadwick informs me.

My heart is in my mouth. I can hardly breathe. I don't want to hear it. I can't cope. I can't.

I put my mobile down, tears pouring down my face. I'm dizzy with emotion. They've found her – and him. At last he's made a mistake, a mistake that has saved my beautiful princess.

THE DARK PLACE

It's so dark in here. I reach out a hand and it touches something soft and squidgy. I was frightened when they first put me in here. I can't remember when they did, but I've been here ages now. It's not a bad prison really. In fact, it's quite warm and I get everything I need. But I'd still rather be outside. I suppose it's my punishment. Mum said I was bad, but I'm not. Not really. And I should know. I've had plenty of time to think about it. That's all you can do in here. Think, think, think.

I'm Daniel, by the way. Daniel Bradman, 15 years old. There's nothing remarkable about me. I'm just your average school kid who hates all teachers and the older generation who reckon they know everything about everything. I don't like poncy boy bands or vegetables. But I do like Kylie. She's not bad for an old bird. I like kebabs and smoking, too. Though don't tell my mum. She smokes at least a hundred fags a day, but she would string me up by my boot laces if she ever caught me having a puff.

Mum likes a drink now and then, too. I hate it. Alcohol. My best mate, Pete, and me were going to the school disco. Mum was out at bingo, so we raided the drinks cabinet, if you can call two bottles of gin and a can of lager a drinks cabinet. The lager slipped down nicely, but the gin tasted like polish. And yes, I have tasted polish. It's one of those daft things you do as a kid. Still, the gin did the trick.

It was quite a laugh at first. Even geeky Georgina

looked sexy, swaying her hips to the latest Dua Lipa had to offer. It was still a laugh when I fell over. But when I threw up all over the deputy headmaster, it all went a bit wrong. Mum wasn't too impressed when I got a Saturday detention.

I know I disappoint her. She'd like me to do well at school and do something with my life. Dad was a waster. Even he admits that. He mucked around and left school as soon as he could. He's never been able to hold down a job for longer than a few months. I don't want to be like him. I do try hard at school, but I can't seem to concentrate for long. My mind starts drifting to football. I love Man U, though it isn't the same club it used to be. They used to be the best in the world. There my mind goes again. I can't help myself, so I suppose I am like my dad in that way.

Mum's different. She got ten G.C.S.E.s. She wanted to be a librarian, but then she met Dad. I don't know why she gave up her dreams for him. Well, I do. She's told me often enough.

"I went to an all-girls' school. We didn't know anything about boys. Your dad was a vision, like Tom Cruise, only here in Wiltshire. I didn't know about sex and where it led. I did when you came along nine months later."

Mum's parents were furious – 'so disappointed in our daughter'. Mum and Dad got married after that and rented a tatty little flat. Mum worked at the local supermarket in the day and she got a cleaning job in the evening. Dad did nothing – except drink, smoke and bet away any money Mum made. Dad did a job last year – a robbery on a post office. He's been in prison for ten months. I don't want to be like my dad.

I want to be like my mum.

She went a bit funny when Dad was first put away. She kept crying and screaming. I thought she'd gone round the bend. She fell to the floor and banged her head. There was blood everywhere and she didn't wake up for ages, not even when the ambulance arrived.

When she came home, I made a promise to her. I told her I would look after her and I would study hard and get a good job so we could have a nice house and a decent car, instead of the wreck outside.

I thought I'd kept my promise, but I can't have. I wouldn't be in here otherwise. I didn't want to do it, but I didn't have any choice.

"Billy's got a Scirocco. Coming for a ride in it tonight?" Pete asked.

Billy is his brother. He's a year older than us, but he looks about twenty-five. He's big trouble. He's nicked loads of cars as well as stuff from shops. He hasn't been caught yet, but I steer clear of him if I can.

"Scirocco? He's slipping, Pete. Next time he'll be pinching scooters," I laughed.

"Coward. You're a bloody coward, Bradman," Pete yelled at me.

His eyes were like slits and he looked just like his brother. So I did it. I told Mum Pete and me were going to study for our French exam together. Her raised eyebrows told me she didn't believe me, but I went anyway.

Billy and Pete were waiting at the end of the lane, the one near the woods. Pete had shaved his head and looked even more like his brother. My stomach felt like I'd eaten ten kebabs before doing a hundred sit-ups.

I wondered what I was doing there. Why did I hang round with Pete? I was sure he had started nicking stuff, too. As I walked towards them, I looked into their eyes. There was something there: madness, evil, drugs. Whatever it was I wanted out of there. I could have been at home watching *Eastenders* with Mum and some other kid could be getting into trouble.

"Look at him, Pete. He's scared. What an ignoramus," Billy jeered. "This ain't roundabout and swing stuff, Bradman."

"Give me the keys then." I stuck out my chest, drawing myself up to my full five feet six inches.

He laughed at me. They both did. I was going to run, but then I saw the knife. Billy twirled it round and round like an expert swordsman, through one finger then another.

"I ain't letting you anywhere near the steering wheel of this beauty," Billy said, pointing the blade at me. "In, kid. Now."

I did as he ordered and got in the back. I reached for the seat belt, knowing I would need it.

"Aww, little baby wants to use a seat belt. Want a dummy, too?" Pete was gaining in confidence.

I let the seat belt go and it snapped back into place.

Billy threw Pete the keys and Pete clambered into the driver's seat. He flashed me a big grin, his eyes almost aglow. As we lunged forward and I was nearly catapulted into the front seat, I knew he'd done this before. I held onto the front headrest, my knuckles white as he zigzagged through the traffic, giving the horn a blast at everything in his way. I closed my eyes and wondered if I wished hard enough, somehow it wouldn't be happening to me.

"Get a move on, Pete. I'm meeting Spam at eight and I'm getting desperate. You up for a snort, kid?" Billy said, manic eyes turning to me.

Waves of sickness churned round and round in my stomach. I'd never done drugs before. Dad's brother died of an overdose when he was seventeen. I wouldn't ever, ever touch them.

The knife glinted in the final show of sunlight. But then everything changed. It was a bit strange really. I can't remember much about it. One minute we were zooming along and the next, the car seemed to try and take off. I don't recall it landing. There was a loud snap and screams, lots and lots of screams. I'm sure I heard Pete shouting at me, too. I think he was trying to tell me to wake up. And when I did wake up, I was in here, all alone.

I wish they would let me see Mum. I miss her. I want to hug her and tell her I'm sorry and that I'm a good boy really. Most of all, I want to tell her I love her. But I can't do any of that. All I can do is eat, sleep and think. But it doesn't matter. Mum knows.

My hands are touching each other. They've grown again. It's very strange, this growing thing. And eating. It's not like normal eating, not with a knife and fork. The food's pretty bland and there's always loads of vegetables. When I get out of here I'm going to have a curry.

Something is happening. There's a funny light ahead. I don't know why, but I have to push my head down near it. I can hear grunting and screaming. It's a woman. She's in agony.

She's shouting at someone, "It's all your fault. I hate you!"

"There, there, love, just one more push," a man's voice now.

I can't remember. I can't remember anything. I can't even remember my own name. Something is forcing me forward. It's time for me to go. And all I can do is cry.

ACKNOWLEDGEMENTS

My heart-felt thanks goes to Charlotte Newton, for once again designing the most amazing book cover and for bringing my book to life.

An enormous thank you to The Writers Bureau for being the first to make me believe that I could become a writer and for their unwavering support over the years.

And to all my family and friends who have supported me and encouraged me to follow my writing dream.

ABOUT THE AUTHOR

Esther Chilton has always loved words and writing, but she started out working with figures in a bank. She was on an accelerated training programme and studying banking exams, which meant she didn't have time for writing, so it wasn't long before it was a thing of the past – or so she thought. Her love affair with writing ignited again when she had a serious injury to her back. It meant she could no longer carry out her job working in the bank and it led her back to writing, which has become a daily part of her life.

She has now been working as a freelance writer for over twenty years, regularly writing articles and short stories for magazines and newspapers such as *Freelance Market News, Writers' Forum, Writing Magazine, The Guardian, Best of British, The Cat, This England* and *The People's Friend* to name a few.

Winner of several competitions, including those run by *Writing Magazine and Writers' News,* Esther has also had the privilege of judging writing competitions.

The Storm is her third book of short stories. You can find her first two books, *The Siege* and *A Walk in the Woods,* on Amazon.

As well as working as a freelance writer, she has branched out into the exciting world of copywriting, providing copy for sales letters, brochures, leaflets, web pages, slogans and emails.

Esther loves writing but enjoys helping others just

as much, which she achieves in her role as a tutor for *The Writers Bureau*. She feels like a proud parent when one of her students has a piece of writing published. Some of them have gone on to become published authors and have achieved great success.

In addition to tutoring, Esther is a freelance copyeditor offering an editing, guidance and advice service for authors and writers. She works with writers on all aspects of writing, including novels, non-fiction books, articles and short stories. You can find out more about it by going to her website: http://estherchilton.co.uk/editing-proofreading-and-advice-service/

If you would like Esther's help, or would like to know more about what she can do for you, please get in touch: estherchilton@gmail.com

Other links:

Blog: https://estherchilton.co.uk

Twitter: Esther Chilton @esthernewton201

Facebook: https://www.facebook.com/esther.chilton1

LinkedIn: https://www.linkedin.com/in/esther-chilton-a50ba591/